GOOD-LOOKING UGLY

GOOD-LOOKING UGLY
BY ROB D. SMITH

"With an unforgettable protagonist at its core, Rob D. Smith's smartly-crafted **Good-Looking Ugly** moves with the skill and efficiency of the cockfighting heist at its center. Smith's expert balance of rural grit, sharp banter, and complex family relationships marks him as one to watch."
> —**James D.F. Hannah**, Shamus-winning author of **Because the Night**

"**Good Looking-Ugly** is a propulsive, insistent story, rich with wildly flawed characters. It follows a man pushed to the edge, fighting to save the only person he's ever loved, and explores the complexities of family and loyalty with humor and empathy. A compelling debut."
> —**Meagan Lucas**, author of the Anthony nominated collection, **Here in the Dark**

"Rob D. Smith's raucous debut novel **Good-Looking Ugly** centers on an unforgettable protagonist in the fiercely loyal and fearsomely violent Daniel, who will stop at nothing to protect his family from the Kentucky Fried Mafia. Finger-lickin' good!"
> —**Scott Von Doviak**, author of **Lowdown Road**

"Noted short story writer Rob D. Smith turns his tough-but-witty sensibilities to the novel in his debut, **Good-Looking Ugly**. This is a book that grabs you from the first sentence with its authentic, sharp voice and refuses to let go. A remarkable first effort from an immensely talented writer. Don't sleep on this one."
> —**Bobby Mathews**, Anthony-nominated author of **Magic City Blues**

GOOD LOOKING UGLY

A NOVEL

ROB D. SMITH

Published by **Shotgun Honey Books**

215 Loma Road
Charleston, WV 25314
www.ShotgunHoney.com

Cover by Bad Fido.

First Printing 2024.

ISBN-10: 1-956957-75-8
ISBN-13: 978-1-956957-75-4

9 8 7 6 5 4 3 2 1   24 23 22 21 20 19

*To my mother and father
who have taught me more about life
than they will ever know*

GOOD-LOOKING UGLY

ONE

DON'T SMILE AT PRETTY WOMEN OR BABOONS.

Daniel had learned that first lesson early in life at daycare when he smiled at his first babysitter. The second lesson came from the caretaker job at the Louisville Zoo the judge lined up for him. The baboons shrieked and threw twigs and leaves back onto the dirt floor Daniel had just raked clean. It didn't raise his hackles. They were just acting to their nature. He was the interloper in their habitat. He might have done the same thing if someone tried to clean up the empty soda cans and magazines in his den.

He'd begun to rake up the mess again carefully adding this litter to the pile in his garbage bag. The large male baboon named Targus rushed up and pulled at his bag then ran away to his troop. Daniel smiled to himself but was careful not to show it to the baboons. They saw a flash of teeth as aggression. He never liked to share his gap-toothed smile with anyone.

"Brown! Hey, what did I tell you about working in the pen with the animals?" Daniel's boss Roger yelled at him from the cart path never getting off his electric jitney.

He stopped raking. "They don't bother me."

"It's more protection for them than you. They don't need to see your ugly puss. Might keep them from making more babies." His boss laughed at his joke.

"Now get out of there and clean the giraffe cage. The keepers got them empty. And quit messing with the animals. You ain't Dr. Dolittle." With that order, Roger gunned his jitney away from the baboon exhibit and off to hassle another groundskeeper at the zoo. His boss' joke didn't sting Daniel. He heard a million about his appearance from people growing up. Most from his own family.

Daniel gathered his tools and the garbage bag to leave. He went behind the fake mountain wall to the door painted a sandy stone color. Checking to make sure no hairy Houdinis were behind or above him, he slipped out of the pen into the secondary service room. He followed protocols noting there were no primates but him in the room. He signed a hanging clipboard and left through a rear door. The afternoon sun pierced down heating up every surface of the zoo. Rainbow prisms formed along the automatic grass sprinklers misting.

Daniel put his gas station sunglasses on. Blocky and black to hide the sun and his bulging eyes. Despite the brilliant sun in the cloudless sky, it was cool enough to wear his hooded sweatshirt and for that he was thankful. His glasses, hood up, and finally, his thick beard were all the layers he could add to keep people from gawking at his face.

The zoo was different. At least with the animals. They didn't judge him on his appearance. Only his behavior. This was a nice change of pace from day-to-day reality. There weren't any warthogs or warthogs posting pictures of him on social media.

His court ordered therapist Doctor Rhiney said to focus on inner thoughts to resolve outer actions. You control your reality, not other people. She had given him a list of books to read that would help affirm a more positive outlook. Some of the books hooked him. Most seemed like redundant hippy crapola. He was willing to try anything to get control of his hair-trigger temper. His looks and his anger had brought him to the precipice of a stint in prison if he violated any terms of his probation. Hold a steady job and no more fighting were the two non-negotiables.

He put his full bag in the waste can on the back of his jitney. His work cart wasn't as good as Rogers's. It was a holdover from the seventies and had three wheels instead of four. And that front wheel had a mind of its own. You had to hold firm on the steering yoke or you might wipe out a group of zoo patrons. Daniel liked this job too much to lose it.

He got to the giraffe indoor pen in good time. Foot traffic was light. In late September all the kids were in school. Occasionally there would be a field trip to the zoo from one of the grade schools but none this week. Kids don't have much of a filter and would just blurt out how ugly Daniel was. Kids weren't his favorite but as long as he stuck to the back of the pens he could avoid them.

Adults didn't outright comment on his looks unless they were waiting too long in the grocery checkout line. They didn't have good enough poker faces to hide their revulsion. Just giant kids with a little bit of a filter. You hold the keys to your reality. You alone. He forgot what book he read that from. Another self-help guide Dr. Rhiney loaned him.

He went inside the pen. A different funky odor than the baboons invaded his nostrils. The zoo could keep three giraffes in corresponding compartments. The giraffes get moved out the back through a fairly narrow trough system to an open exhibit but the ceilings in the pen were a tremendous height. The floor-to-ceiling light-ing kept very few shadows from appearing. It also shone every speck of scat and piss the long-legged mammals dropped to the floor. Daniel cleaned the enclosure almost twice a day.

There was a large glass viewing area for visitors at two of the pens. The third pen had wide polished bars that the people could interact with the giraffe. As he washed down the walls with the high-pressure hose, a zoo docent named Molly escorted an elderly couple through the interior. He had seen her around all Summer. She said something to the couple and they all laughed.

He turned his back on them and sprayed the floor.

Giraffe poo and other detritus broke free and floated to the drainage hole. He expected they were laughing at him. They all laughed at him except the pious ones. Their pity was gasoline on his rage. Another hardening of another layer. He heard something pecking.

Molly tapped her keys on the plexiglass to get his attention. She pointed to the third pen with the bars so he turned off his hose and went over there to the bars. She waited with a big smile hugging her computer tablet.

"Hey, Daniel. Do you know when the giraffes will be back inside? The Comstocks are big donors and would like to pet them if they could."

He wore his dark sunglasses inside. Even wearing them he still couldn't bring himself to make eye contact with those blue eyes. They should make an exhibit for him between the African vultures and the hyenas. Her lips moved but he hadn't heard a word she was saying.

"…like working here or is cleaning up after everyone a pain in the butt?" She made small talk while his imagination ran amok again. Have to bring that up in his weekly session with Dr. Rhiney too.

"I don't mind it. It's mostly quiet," he said.

"Quiet? Lord, I can hear the macaws on the other side of the zoo." She smiled.

"I think of them as my own little animal orchestra." Daniel forgot himself and returned her smile. His wide picket fence teeth. You don't smile at baboons or pretty women. He knew better.

A polite laugh but he caught her facial tic. "I'll bring

them back around four. Think at least one giraffe will be back by then?"

"Sure. I'll say something to Curt. Nice speaking with you Molly." He waved to her back.

She had already headed back to the old moneyed couple. He picked up the wide broom handle squeegee and pushed any water on the floor toward the drainage hole. His grip tightened on the wood pole. The pole began to quiver and Daniel snapped it in half like a dry twig. He checked to see if anyone had noticed then took the broken squeegee out back to his cart and threw it in his waste bin.

He slipped a water bottle out of his cooler and took a pull. His hands trembled. He rarely vocalized his anger. It usually erupted into some kind of physical manifestation. He was getting better. He didn't show his anger in front of people anymore. And since his last court date, he hadn't struck anyone yet when his temper flared. He was one percent better every day.

Daniel felt eyes on him. He could always tell when someone was watching. Judging him on his looks on society's scales of attractiveness. It was a weight to bear. And it made him angry. So angry. He checked around and saw a couple of visitors walking but no one looking in his direction. He swept left and saw the lion Mako narrowing his eyes at him from his fake stone butte.

TWO

DANIEL LEFT THE ZOO AT FIVE. He worked mostly the day shift but would pick up a second shift if someone needed him to. Any overtime was great since this job paid so little. He cut through the parking lot then went across Illinois Ave and started down Grenade Ave to his basement apartment. Tall oak trees lined the street.

He went around back and let himself in the door. He rented this basement apartment from Patricia Elwood. She traveled a lot since her husband died unexpectantly and someone staying in the basement would keep burglars away. She said, "A widow must constantly stay on the move or be brought down by potential suitors". The eccentric woman took a shine to Daniel and gave him a good rate plus the privacy he sought. She rarely asked questions and only romanticized her past.

He turned on the lights. It was a mostly finished basement with an open floor plan one large exterior window and a couple of little windows near the ceiling. The bathroom was small but had a shower. The bedroom was just as tiny but pitch dark when he needed some shut-eye. A kitchenette with a microwave, a hot plate, and a sink. His TV wasn't big either but it did the trick. The widow Elwood did let him hang a heavy bag in the corner where he also kept some kettlebells. Besides Dr. Rhiney, exercise was his best therapy.

His other prized possession was his bookshelf. Used paperbacks took up two-thirds of it while DVDs used up the other third of the space. On top of the shelves were three wrestling masks on Styrofoam mannequin heads. Two elaborate luchador replica masks and one mask from the defunct Mid-South Wrestling Federation. A replica of the original all-white Medics mask.

He put his keys, sunglasses, and basic cell phone in a bowl on top of a small refrigerator that served as an end table next to his couch. He turned on his TV and flipped to the El Rey channel. Ms. Elwood had the full cable package which was an added benefit of the apartment. He got a Sprite out of the fridge and plopped down on the couch. He had just kicked his feet up on his cracked leather couch when there was a knock at his door.

Ms. Elwood just left on her latest west coast jaunt. And no one else had ever knocked on his door. Not even the Jehovah's Witnesses. He went to the door and saw someone trying to peek through his blinds. They knocked again. Daniel jerked the door open. A young blond woman in black worn leggings and a white tank top was caught in mid-knock and he had forgotten his sunglasses. He instinctively tried to cover his monstrous eyes.

"Danny Boy!" she said. The stranger rushed through the door and gave him a big hug.

He had raised his arms overhead when she hugged him careful not to spill the Sprite he held. Only his cousin Jayla called him Danny Boy. He awkwardly brought his arms down and draped her shoulders in his attempt at a hug. He hadn't seen her in ten years. Since that last family picnic dust-up when his mother showed her ass for the penultimate time.

She stepped back and tugged his beard playfully. "Grown a full-on man's beard huh?"

He took her hand from his beard. No anger in the movement. Just affection. He didn't realize he had missed her till just this moment. "I couldn't grow a mask so this was the next best thing."

She punched him in the arm. "Knock off that Negative Nancy routine and invite me in."

"You already are in."

He turned so she could see his place in all its glory. She swept through like the hurricane he remembered from childhood. Jayla inspected and touched everything once. She made sharp jokes and observations. Opened his fridge, checked out the bathroom, and laughed at his displayed wrestling masks finally her tour came to an end at his heavy bag. She did a little Muhammed Ali two-step and jabbed it.

"Ow, that's solid leather, Danny boy." She flicked her hand back and forth.

"What are you doing here?"

She feigned offense. "I drove all this way to see my favorite cousin and I don't even get offered a drink."

"There's Sprite in the fridge and tap water from the sink."

She snatched the Sprite from his hand and took a pull. She gave a dramatic satisfied sound and then sat down on his couch. She patted the space next to her.

"Take a load off. You've had a hard day cleaning up after those critters."

He sat down. "Have you been watching me? I thought I felt someone."

"Oh, get over yourself. No one's looking at you. But yeah, I was stalking you at the zoo." She took another drink of the soft drink smiling around the top as she drank.

He laughed for the first time in forever. At least in front of someone else. He relaxed back into the leather couch. "How did you know I worked at the zoo?"

"I tracked your scent. You stink worse than those giraffes and rhinos. It must be your pretentiousness that causes your stench."

"You talked to my mother." Daniel didn't see or talk to his mother much but she was the only one outside of Dr. Rhiney and the court that knew where he worked.

She squinted at him. "I did talk to Aunt Carla. She's still a piece of work. I had to finesse her."

He said, "Cheap bourbon?"

"Heaven Hill. The elixir of truth. She sang like a Pointer Sister."

She looked shocked that he corrected her but that gave in to her famous ear-to-ear smile. Her energy always spun him around. She was intoxicating. He felt alive and in the flow with her. In his mind, they were kids running through Grandpa's farm chasing hens from their hidden hay bale nests. They would take the eggs and throw them at the sows in the hog pen. A day would end with them lying on their backs near the soybean field. Stars and fire-flies competed for best overall twinkles.

His face must have beamed because Jayla was quietly looking at him with warmth in her eyes. He gave her a rough but genuine hug this time. After he let go, she tussled his long hair.

"I missed us, Daniel."

"I didn't know it but so did I"

She was sitting cross-legged on his couch. Patting his knee, she said, "Let's go get some real drinks. My treat."

The magic slipped from Daniel's eyes. He leaned away from her and pulled his hood up. "I don't know about that. I don't go out much."

She noticed his retreat. "Come on it will do you good to hang out with humans instead of just animals."

"Animals like me."

"People will too. If you let some get close, they may be cool like me."

"They may be assholes.

"I can't correct you there. This planet is populated with

ninety-one percent assholes. Let's go see if any bars in Louisville have the nine percent good guys."

Danial slouched over and exhaled heavily. He hadn't had an incident in two months. Aside from the occasional destruction of minor property like today's squeegee and the hole he kicked in a bathroom door at the Waffle House. She took his hands.

"I know you're scared but I'm here. Copilot supreme."

He laughed. "You're the little person on my shoulder? Are you telling me to light the fire or telling me to stamp out the fire?"

She leaned on him and slung her arm around his shoulder. "Bit of both I'm afraid. Now let's get out of here."

She pulled on him to get off the couch and he relented. They were out the door when he stopped walking. "I forgot something. Be right back."

He ran in and grabbed his sunglasses out of the bowl. He put them on and went back out to Jayla. She shook her head.

"Alright Hollywood, my car is right down the street. Where do you want to go?"

He pointed up the block to his right. "Oskars is two blocks up. We can walk there."

"Sweet, we won't need a designated driver."

Daniel thought, no more ominous words had ever been uttered.

THREE

THEY WERE TWO BEERS IN when Daniel started to unhunch his shoulders. It was a wonder he never cramped up from all the anxious tightening and releasing of certain muscles while he was in public. He never could loosen up when he was exposed. But right now, at this moment with his cousin, he felt normal if not relaxed. He was thankful.

Oskar's was a bar run by an eclectic couple who had a restaurant in the trendy downtown area called NuLu. They lived in the Camp Taylor neighborhood and wanted someplace for the locals to drink and have some sliders. Daniel had read about them in the local alternative weekly paper. He had never struck up a conversation with the owners when he picked the gourmet sliders to go. And he never would. It wasn't his way to start small talk with strangers.

It was after ten now on a Wednesday and it had thinned out a little. Most people sat at the bar made of polished Spanish Oak. Daniel noticed the three big guys in work coats near the end towards the bathroom entrance.

Jayla yammered incessantly. She caught him up on uncles and aunts he hadn't heard about or seen in years. The circus came to Loretto and she wrestled a bear for money. The bear won of course so Jayla snuck back in later got it drunk and let it loose. That he had heard about on the news but didn't know it was her. He should have assumed.

He laughed so hard his physical body got out of control and he knocked a beer glass from their table. The loud shatter brought everyone's attention to their table. On him. Up went his hoodie. He shrunk into himself. Willing his mass smaller and smaller.

A waitress came over with a bus bin to clean up the broken glass. She looked at Daniel. "Don't worry sugar. Happens all the time."

Jayla grasped his forearm as soon as the waitress left. "Don't do that. There is nothing wrong with you."

"I can't help how I look."

"You look fine. But it's not about what I think or anyone else. It's what you feel inside."

He nodded slightly. "My therapist says *I* control my responses. That outside stimulus is not in my control but my emotions and how *I* react are."

"Is this therapy part of your court order?"

"Mother told you."

"Heaven Hill is powerful medicine. Aunt Carla mentioned you had some trouble with the law. Beat up some guys at a gas station."

He held up his hands. "It wasn't my first arrest for assault. Once the court sees my face, I get a little pity and a slap on the wrist. But this one was on video and made the evening news. Had to make an example."

"You were on TV? How did you not do any jail time?"

He grinned. "A public defender who was hell on wheels. Got the video thrown out but I'm on probation. And I have therapy with Dr. Rhiney until she signs off."

"Dr. Rhiney? She sounds hot. Do you have a crush on her? You do, don't you?"

Daniel blushed. "She's a good doctor. Gave me some pills for anxiety too."

"You were always a sucker for women in authority." She drank down the rest of her beer. "Damn these craft beers are expensive but they'll knock you on your ass. I gotta pee. Be right back." She got up and went towards the bathrooms. Daniel reached out to stop her then nervously brought his hand back.

Without Jayla at the table, the sounds were too sharp. The lights were too bright. He caught side-eye glances from his peripheral vision. He felt like a raw nerve exposed. Follow your breath he heard Dr. Rhiney say in his head. She taught him a breathing technique the Navy Seals used to calm themselves down in combat. He altered and counted his breaths in a certain sequence. And damn if he didn't calm down a bit.

Someone touched his arm. It wasn't the waitress. One of the men from the bar had come over. He had short-cropped red hair. His cheeks and nose were wind burned. His two pals stood behind as backup. Daniel lost count of what breath he was on.

"You planning to rob this place?" asked the big man.

Daniel scooted out of the booth instinctively. His hands went up. "What are you talking about?"

"Dressed all in black with your big glasses on. Hood up. Acting all twitchy. I get the feeling you're casing the joint." He got in Daniel's space. Close enough so Daniel could smell stale sweat and fetid beer breath

Daniel felt his neck flush and the urge to lash out rising. He settled on his breath again as he stepped back creating space. "I'm just here drinking with my cousin."

The redhead snatched the glasses off his face before he could react. Daniel's protruding bug eyes were on full display. The two guys behind the redhead started to laugh. The man holding his glasses turned and snarled at them. "Shut the fuck up."

He handed the glasses back to Daniel. His expression softened. "I'm drunk. Sorry man. We'll leave you alone."

Pity was worse than ridicule. Daniel's neck burned like a California brush fire. He put his glasses on the table then swung a ridge hand into the big redhead's windpipe. The guy started barking like a seal. Before his two buddies could react, Daniel planted a solid push kick into the wheezing redhead's stomach sending him back into his two drunk friends. They all toppled over themselves and some chairs.

Daniel rushed to inflict more harm on the fallen men. Someone grabbed his sleeve as he was raising his boot to stomp. "Stop!"

He almost swung and hit Jayla with an open hand. She handed him his glasses. He put them on and the heat from his neck flushed away. The three large men lay prone on the floor. Shocked a touch sober by the acceleration of the smaller man's violence. Jayla went to the bar and handed the bartender some cash.

She tugged him by his sleeve. "Let's roll Danny. Our money's no good here anymore."

Daniel followed but checked for cameras on his way out of Oskar's door. This was why he didn't go to bars or out much socially. He didn't need any more videos of his bad acts to get out in the world. He doubt he would sleep all night worrying that his probation officer or the judge would find out he slipped up again. What would he tell Dr. Rhiney? He knew with a little shame that he would lie to her for the first time.

Sitting on Daniel's worn leather sofa, the two cousins drank some bourbon Jayla bought at Walgreens on the way home. He had never been a big drinker and with his prescribed pills regimen, he was gassed. Jayla seemed her same kinetic self. She had a vape pen that she would take a drag on and then release a cloud of mint vapor into his apartment every few minutes.

He cast his head back as far as the couch cushion would let him. "Where have you been?"

She knew what he meant. "I've been in Loretto this whole time. Never left. You could have come to see this country mouse anytime you wanted."

"The TARC bus doesn't go all the way to Nelson County."

She vaped again. "I ain't pushing. It's not like I came looking for you either. What's wrong with us?"

He was so drowsy. "I know we got a better chance of fixing ourselves together."

"I'm glad to hear you say that because I got something to ask you. A big whopping favor."

His eyes were shut and his head lolled further into relaxation. "I could tell but do me a favor. Wait till morning. I don't want to ruin my sleep with nightmares."

"No problemo. It's only my life going down the shitter. But don't worry your sleepy little self. I can put my sanity on hold for…"

Daniel reached out his hand. Fingers searching for her touch then slowly dropping on his stomach. "That's my country mouse. Night."

The last thing he remembered was Jayla draping his army blanket over him.

FOUR

DANIEL'S HEAD HURT. He could feel one vein pulsing in his head. A painful metronome. His tongue was dry but coated. What the hell happened to him? Then he smelt fried eggs. He didn't have any eggs in his fridge. A girl hummed When I Come Around by Green Day. He turned his bleary eyes towards his kitchenette.

Jayla scrambled eggs on his hot plate. He wrapped a blanket around himself and went over to inspect. Some crispy bacon was on a paper towel-lined plate. The towel soaked up the residual fat. Two coffee cups from Bean, the local shop up the street.

She noticed him. "Hey sleepyhead, the right one is yours."

He picked up the warm paper cup. "You went out?"

"I couldn't sleep and you were all out of…well, everything. I got some milk, juice, eggs, bacon, bread and saw that coffee place near Kroger's. I got your coffee black."

He smelled the aromatic brew and then took a soul-warming sip. "How did you know I like it without cream or sugar?"

She bumped him with her hip. "Bitter is your spirit animal."

"I'm not bitter." He pouted.

"Okay, Bitter McBitter." She slid the scrambled eggs onto a plate. "Okay get a couple more plates for us to eat on."

He said, "You have already used all my plates. I have a bowl and a big soup mug."

"You need some honing of your rough edges kiddo. I'll take the mug."

They scooped the eggs into his bowl and her mug, stuck a couple of bacon strips into the eggs then went to his couch to eat. The richness of the eggs cooked in bacon fat made Daniel nearly swoon. His arteries may be clogging up but that was a price worth paying. He thanked her for breakfast.

"Don't thank me too soon. I have a huge favor to ask."

He chased down the eggs with the dark roasted coffee. "I can barely keep my head above water. How much help could I be."

"I need someone I can trust. Someone who will ride off the cliff with me. I don't have many like that in my life. But I used to when we were younger."

"We were kids back then Jayla. Hunting grasshoppers and fending off bullies. I have adult-level bullshit to deal with now."

"Aren't you tired of living like this? Living with two plates and no food in the fridge. No money. No freedom. Being scared of the ticking bomb in your head. When will you be free?"

"I've been working on it. Takes time to build a life. Doesn't sprout out fully grown with a house, a wife, and three little kids."

"If you could take the express lane to the top, would you?"

"Just spit it out."

"I need you to help me rob a cockfighting match."

"That sounds about par for your course." He drank his coffee.

"What's that mean?"

"No way will I help you rob a cotton-picking chicken fight. Or knock off a gas station. Or run counterfeit money up from Florida. N O no."

She leaped off the couch and started pacing in front of him. "I turn to you in my hour of need and you make fun of me. Me."

"Your schemes always entail me being the fall guy."

"Bullshit, I never let you take the blame alone."

"No, but you drug me down with you. That was okay back then. Now I'm already in Dutch. One more strike and I'll do real-time."

"No one is going to get caught, Daniel."

Daniel got up and threw his breakfast in his trash can.

He wasn't hungry anymore. His back was turned to her. "I think you better leave."

Jayla said, "You're my only hope Obi-Wan Kenobi."

Damn her. He started to laugh but when he turned, he saw her tears. He approached her slowly. "Tell me the truth."

Jayla's tale of woe began three years ago. It had started as love or so she thought. She muled marijuana to neighboring states for this dealer named Grassman. That wasn't a nickname. Some people are just destined to live up to their names. Anyway, she delivered the product in the county one time to Archie Mudd who sold it to his guests. He ran the Bluegrass Sportsman Club outside Loretto for the Kentucky Fried Mafia. The Bluegrass Sportsman Club was a fancy name for a cockfighting association.

Archie took a shine to Jayla. And Jayla liked the attention from such a handsome if diminutive outlaw such as Archie. He had some power and she had some moxie. She gave up the mule business and started working with Archie at the club. On a hundred-acre wooded plot, Archie had built a cockfighting arena that's stands held 3,000 people with the help of his brother Johnny Mudd, the leader of KFM. Attendees came from almost every state in the nation. Some even came from the Philippines, Mexico, Puerto Rico, and the Dominican Republic. Last year she saw a sheik from the Emirates.

Things were good. She was making good money with Archie. Less chance of getting caught by the law. Hell, they hired local police and correction guards for security during events. She witnessed a judge and other government officials at the matches. Archie kicked money up to his brother Johnny Mudd and the KFM but he still brought home 1.2 million a year. Things were good in the Bluegrass for Jayla and her beau.

Archie had always had a temper. He was a short man but thick. He would fly off the handle at other employees but never her. A rumor started that she was cheating on him. He said he didn't believe it but she could see the gossip worm burrowing into his brain. He became jealous and possessive. His right-hand man Billy followed her whenever she left on an errand. Jayla figured when Archie saw there was no hanky panky going on he would let it go.

Archie got darker the more he couldn't catch her doing something she wasn't. His obsession with control might have led to the first punch. The rest was just plain evil. He would tan her legs with a belt. She went to the emergency room after one violent punch to the stomach. He had cracked her rib. The nurse tried to get her to press charges. She just wanted to get out of there.

She tried to leave Archie one night. Just taking the necessities. Billy caught her and brought her back. This time he wasn't worried about leaving a mark for others to see. He gave her a black eye, busted lips, and a concussion. He told her now she could leave and never come back. This time she told the nurse she wanted to press charges. The county deputy that showed up had worked at the club.

She left the hospital without pressing charges. Instead, she went to the county district attorney. He listened and promised he would look into her case. Three days later a DEA taskforce team broke into her small apartment and found over eight ounces of pot. Too much for recreational use only. After her speedy trial, the district attorney that she asked for help asked for the maximum penalty. The judge complied and gave her a $1000 fine and one year in jail. She got out in six months for good behavior. That was a month ago.

"You want to hurt your ex by stealing his money?" He sat on his couch with his elbows on his knees.

"I want to decimate him. Burn him to ashes but I'll settle on getting enough money to start new somewhere else." She paced back and forth in front of him.

He said, "You can just leave and go somewhere else now."

She slapped her forehead. "I can? Well, why didn't I think about that before? Oh yeah, 'cause I have a felony on me and I'm still on parole for six months."

"Well then ride out the six months. Keep your nose clean and stay away from your ex. Then leave. Come to Louisville. Stay with me."

She paused her pacing by his only real window. "I won't make it six months. I came home one day from the factory job my parole officer got me. Billy had his legs kicked up on my coffee table while watching a basketball game on TV. Wherever I go I see law dogs that helped

Archie out. I'm being gaslighted. Trying to get me to break parole or maybe they will fake my suicide. I'm at the end of a noose either way."

"Jayla I'll help you any way I can. But robbing Archie with all his connections doesn't make sense."

She split the blinds with her fingers and peered outside. "It's just in Nelson and the surrounding counties. Once we get the money, I can leave. I met a person while incarcerated that knows some people who can get us across the border for a price."

"Mexico?"

She let go of the blinds. "Un uh. Canada. I'll head up north."

"How much money are you talking about?" He felt like bluegill falling for a rubber worm.

She came over and sat close to him on the couch. "The real money comes from the gambling at the mains. We could walk out with close to a million dollars."

"Just walk out. I bet these aren't the nicest people we will be stealing from. They could have a long reach."

"And that's why we will pin it on Archie. He'll be on the hook and the bigger badder fish will eat him not us."

And this bluegill will already be in the frying pan, he thought. "This is insane. We just can't rob a cockfighting club. I don't know Jayla."

"I ain't saying it will be a cakewalk but we can do it."

"Sounds like we need an army to break in."

She pushed him with her shoulder. "We'll need some help but I got us covered."

"You already have other people involved in this?"

"A small crew. You would make four."

He said, "Who else you got?"

"An inside man Carl Donger. He's still working there but he's tired of eating Archies shit."

Daniel opened his hands waiting for the other name. She said, "Meg is our wheelman. Wheel woman. I met her when I was inside. She's fierce."

"Is she the one who knows how to get you into Canada?"

She nodded. "She has the experience we need."

Daniel got up and poured his cold coffee into the sink then threw the cup into the waste bin. He went over to his heavy bag and leaned on it. "When is this big cockfight?"

"Next weekend."

"Seems a little rushed to me. Shouldn't we watch Archie and the place before we do this?"

She paced over to his heavy bag opposite Daniel's position. "It's the Super Bowl of Cockfights, Danny. It's now or wait another year. I won't make another year."

"I can't mess up this court stuff, Jayla. I slip up and I serve a stretch."

She nudged the bag with her shoulder. "Can you call in sick? Say it's late-stage swine flu."

"I could call in sick for the week. I can't skip my weekly session with Dr. Rhiney."

"What day do you meet?"

He said, "Mondays."

She clapped her hands. "No problem. Monday after your session we drive out to Loretto. Five days later on Saturday, we knock off Archie's club. Sunday everyone splits up. And Monday you go back to work and make goo-goo eyes at Dr. Rhiney."

"You are certifiable."

"I need your help Hollywood. Just one last time. Then you'll never see me again."

Daniel hadn't thought about that. They had just briefly reconnected and it felt good to laugh and be loose again. Once Jayla was gone the brightness would be too. There was comfort in his dull daily routine. No country outlaws shooting at him for one. No chance for his probation revoked. She needed him though. And he had never been needed before.

She was staring at him from the side of the heavy bag. He looked down at the concrete floor. Her nervous energy vibrated the bag. He looked back up at her.

"Say yes. Yes. Yes. Yes."

He stepped away from the bag and stroked his beard. "I need time to think about it?"

Jayla smiled. "Really? Okay."

"I need the time alone."

"To think. I'll go sightseeing for a little bit. Maybe head to a sports bar and catch the Wildcat's game. Give me a call when you're done thinking." She made air quotes when she said thinking.

His hands cover his face. "Jayla."

"I'm going." She got her denim jacket and walked to the door. "Whatever you decide, I still love you. But just think hard on this because I need your ass to save my ass."

She walked out and left the door not all the way closed. Danial popped up and locked the door behind her. He took a deep breath and smelled mint vapor, bacon grease, and hot buttered eggs. He would spend the day trying to talk himself out of helping Jayla. Nothing good would come of it. If they didn't get killed trying to rob the place, they would probably get caught by the law.

He cleaned up the mess his cousin had made fixing them breakfast. Not a lot of items to wash or distract him from his decision. This was going to be a long day. He dried his last bowl and put it on the rack that acted as his cupboard. He exhaled, went over, and opened the door.

Jayla stood in the door frame with her hand on her cocked hip. "I can't believe you kept me waiting this long.

FIVE

"WE NEED TO CONTROL THEM. Of course, we'll have guns."

Daniel said, "I don't think I can shoot someone."

"But you can bite a chunk out of them? I don't see where your line is."

He winced. "You saw the news footage?"

She had a big Styrofoam cup of Mountain Dew full of pebble ice. She took a big suck on the straw and gave an ah. "I did see you on video fighting like a Viking berserker. And that's the guy I need for the job."

"I can't make that guy appear at will. The violence isn't choreographed. I just do it when I have to."

She shook her head. "I don't buy that. You could run away. You could just suck it up and take the bullying. The name-calling. But you chose to wipe their asses on the concrete that night. You showed your power. And I think you can dial into it when you want, not just at random."

He nodded but didn't believe her. His urge only came up when he was pushed. The fight or flight response never presented itself. All his mind could come up with was maim and destroy. In all honesty, when that trigger was pulled, Daniel didn't remember much. He just crashed like an avalanche filling any space with destruction. He was fortunate he hadn't killed anyone.

"I've never used a gun while I'm like that. I wouldn't want to. I've only ever fired Uncle Mile's rifle. Nothing else."

"You have the basics down. Point and shoot. We'll just have to point it, mostly. Only at a couple of people if we play our cards right. Trust me. The plan is foolproof. I don't want to shoot anyone either." She drew on the straw again until you could hear only air sucking through it. Another satisfied ah.

He hadn't touched his Dr. Pepper yet. His mouth had become very dry talking this over with Jayla. Very dry. He took his first drink and the fountain soda burned his taste buds. He had agreed to help her but everything she said sounded worse than he imagined. He wasn't doing it for the money. He wanted to save his cousin. That's what he told himself. But the chance for violence. He couldn't deny the opportunity to let loose excited him.

"You have everything ready?"

"Yeah, son. We're going to rob the place with or without you. I like our chances better now that you're with me."

"I have to meet with my therapist Monday morning

early. I'll act sick in her office. Then I'll call in sick to the zoo. Establish my alibi."

"We'll leave for Marion County once you hang up the phone." She shimmied her shoulders.

"You know this whole thing could blow up in our faces? How can you be so happy?"

"Just like old times. You carry all the worry and I'll keep woo-hooing. We balance each other out."

She wasn't wrong. Even with this shit show of a heist hanging over his head. Even with him risking jail by skipping town for a week. He had never felt so alive as when he was with Jayla.

Dr. Rhiney's office space was located off Eastern Parkway in a shared medical office building. Dentists, podiatrists, and all other kinds of medical professionals rented space in the 1970's brutalist-style building. A somber place to enter. His therapists' practice was not cold and unwelcoming, however. Warm earth tones from the paint on the wall to the cushions on the couch. No hard edges to put you on guard. She made her space a place of refuge.

He held a pillow from the couch on his lap. Dr. Rhiney tented her hands. "You aren't feeling well?"

He said, "No, not really. I know I have to be here but I didn't feel like getting out of bed today."

"Aches and chills. Are you running a fever?"

He was trying to keep his fake illness to generic symptoms. Nothing to be measured. She was a licensed doctor after all. "I don't think so but I'm a little nauseous."

"Did your mother take care of you when you were sick as a little boy?"

He smiled inside. He knew she would turn this into an opportunity to probe his past. "She usually just told me to stay in my room and not come out till I felt better."

She frowned. "Not even to use the bathroom."

"She gave me a small plastic tub to use."

"And how did that make you feel?"

He shrugged. "You make it sound bad but I didn't know any better. She just didn't want to catch anything from me."

"She isolated you when you were sick. When you were at your worst. I can't help feeling that you've isolated yourself, Daniel. Staying away from others will not solve your aggressive tendencies. True integration of your mind and emotions will depend on your connection to others."

"I lash out at others because I'm pissed at my Mom? That sounds like bargain-basement psychology."

She smiled. "It could be a manifestation of anger towards your mother. It could also be rage you feel at your visage."

He faked a cough. "What am I supposed to do with a face like this? Go into modeling?"

She unfolded her legs and rested her elbows on her knees as she leaned towards him. "You are an intelligent young man. Not classically educated but sharp. You alone control your mind and emotions. It doesn't matter how others perceive you. It matters how you respond. I can't be a model either by the way."

He thought maybe not a model but he bet with those

long legs she had tried her hand at dancing in her youth. She tried levity to connect but she was an attractive woman. Pretty people have no idea of how society bends over backward for them. But try being ugly and destitute from the cradle. See how nice they acted. Dr. Rhiney's lips were moving.

"… you okay? You look a little flushed."

Daniel was a little warm. "Sorry doctor. Guess I'm getting worse."

"Are you going to go to work today? I could call them and verify you aren't well."

"You would do that for me?"

She picked up the phone. "Your well-being is very important to me. I'll just call Mr. Theus and let him know that you are sick. But if you aren't better tomorrow, I suggest seeing a doctor."

He was elated. This added an extra layer to his alibi. "I promise I'll go to the Little Clinic for antibiotics if I don't feel any better."

She held up her hand as she started to speak with the zoo's ER head. Ten minutes later he was in Jayla's late model Ford F-150 headed for Marion County at high speed.

SIX

THEY ARRIVED AT JAYLA'S RENTED trailer home in Loretto. It was in front of a small acreage used for farming. There was an old black barn on the property but no farmhouse. They parked on a gravel driveway next to the trailer. Daniel got his gym bag and followed her up the steps and into the trailer. It smelt stuffy from lack of airflow. She flicked on the lights.

"Mi casa es su casa."

"And I was depressed about my place."

She slapped his arm. "You got some nerve. Your place was Silence of the Lamb territory."

"Ouch. Least I don't have to worry about tornadoes."

She said, "We'll be upgrading our dwellings soon. No tornados in Canada."

"What's up there for you?"

"Space and distance." She went to her kitchen and got an empty glass from the cupboard.

"Where's the bathroom?"

She filled her glass with tap water from the sink. "Back and to the left. Can't miss it."

He dropped his gym bag on the linoleum floor and went to use the bathroom. He noticed the frames on the wall all had motivational speeches. He wondered if they came with the trailer or if Jayla hung them up. Either answer was disturbing. He opened the door to the bathroom and found it didn't close all the way.

He took a long self-conscious piss embarrassed that she could hear him. He hadn't shared living quarters with anybody since his mother kicked him out. That's not completely true. He had a tomcat named Reggie that stayed with him for a while. The cat ran off though. He hoped it wasn't his loud pissing that drove Reggie from his home but he never found out why the feline left. *Wait till Jayla heard him take a crap.*

He freshened up in the sink. Took two pills with a handful of water. Opened the door on the mirror vanity above the sink. Toothpaste and brush. Small bag of floss picks. Some cream for fungus. Advil bottle. A prescription bottle of Paxil. Inspection over, he went back out to the living room where his cousin was watching the news.

She sat on a loveseat for two. A tattered blue canvas lazy-boy recliner was to her left. He sat next to her in front of a TV that took up half the wall of the trailer. The TV likely cost more than this trailer was worth. Jayla caught him shaking his head.

"Yes, I am aware of the cliché hanging on the wall. Let me enjoy something nice for once."

He laughed and looked at the front door then towards the ceiling. She said, "What are you looking for?"

"Just wondering how they squeezed that wide-screen TV into this cracker box?"

"I believe a team of five assembled the TV from parts that were shipped in from South Korea while inside the trailer."

"Smart."

"You left off the ass on that smart."

"It was implied."

She scooted out to the edge of her seat and gave him a serious look. "It's okay to be scared, Daniel."

He said, "Thanks for permission."

"No posturing Hollywood. This is a big risk. You don't have to help me."

He shook his head. "No. We can do this. I'd say it's about time we got what we deserve."

As soon as he finished his sentence, the front door to the trailer slammed open. He jumped up into a ready stance.

"Honey, I'm home!"

A severe-looking woman with a smile on her lips stood wide in the doorway carrying a stuffed plastic grocery bag. She ignored him and took the groceries to the kitchen table. She began to empty them.

"I think I got the almond milk you like. Vanilla?"

Jayla said, "Vanilla's perfect. Thanks."

Daniel went over to the door the woman left wide open and shut it. He took care to set the lock. He turned to appraise the brash woman.

"This is Meg. I told you all about her on the way here." She got up off the loveseat and thrust her hand toward him. "And Meg, this is Daniel."

Daniel went to shake her hand but she kept putting groceries away. She spoke over her shoulder as she stocked the refrigerator. "You're the psycho cousin? The muscle huh?"

Jayla coughed out the water she had just taken a drink from. Daniel's neck started warming up. He stroked his beard and started a deep inhale. She turned from the fridge with an eat shit sneer then busted out laughing. "I'm jerking your chain. Jayla thinks the world of you. Come here."

Meg gave him a monstrous hug. Her arms were thick with muscle. She even hoisted him off the ground a little. Jayla came over to them.

"Isn't she a riot?"

He straightened his sunglasses after Meg let go of him. "Yes. A riot."

Meg opened up the fridge door again and pulled out a chocolate Yoo-hoo. She shook it up, twisted off the top, and tossed the bottle top into an overflowing waste can in the corner. "She shoots she scores."

"Meg played basketball in college. Up in Ohio."

Meg burped loudly after taking a drink of the Yoo-hoo. "Yeah at Corsair College. Near Vermillion."

He said, "Good for you."

Meg went over to the loveseat and took a load off. Jayla followed suit and sat next to her. He was a good little duckling so he sat down in the recliner too. He didn't care about this situation. When Meg put her arm around his cousins' shoulder in a familiar way, he knew Meg was holding back on him. Meg flipped on a football game. Alabama versus Ole Miss.

"Goddamn Bama. SEC is overrated if you ask me, Daniel. I guess you think they are better than the Big Ten too?"

He scratched behind his ear. "I don't follow sports much."

"Hell, I thought when you came out of the womb in Kentucky, they stamped a UK Wildcat brand on your ass."

"Oh, I have one. I just don't follow the Wildcats out of spite for my family."

Jayla leaned over to high-five him. "Amen."

After he returned the high five, she returned to her spot. Meg pulled her close.

"Aren't you two cute?"

He said, "You guys are cute too. Jayla said you met in prison?"

Jayla's eyes sought Daniel. He thought they became stop signs but he didn't relent. "Watch each other's backs? I've been to jail. That's a shit show. I can't imagine prison being any better."

"Women are worse than men sometimes. Why it's good

to circle the wagons so to speak. Find an ally. Jayla and I found we complimented each other. Brains and brawn."

He looked at Jayla and smirked. "You got the brains by default, didn't you?"

"What I have is moxie. And moxie trumps smart any day of the week."

They half-watched the game and got to feel themselves out a little as a trio. Jayla fared the best. She had shared history with both of them. Every time he fell into a comfortable pattern with Jayla, Meg changed to subject to something she was comfortable with. And that seemed like sports, driving, and never going back to prison. He could see Jayla working overtime trying to bridge the gap between him and Meg. He didn't know why he was giving her such a hard time about it. Oh yeah. Meg was an asshole.

Outside had turned to deep dark and the football game ended with Alabama edging out Ole Miss. Meg turned the TV off and stretched. "Time for bed."

With that announcement, she left for the only bedroom in the trailer towards the rear of the place. Jayla got up and handed the throw she had wrapped over him.

"You be okay sleeping on the loveseat?"

He took the throw from her. "Like I'm cheating on my old couch back home but I'll make it work."

She smiled and turned to leave. He sat down on the loveseat and said, "Maybe tomorrow when we're alone, you could explain the nature of your relationship with my new best friend."

She stopped walking and rested her hand on the

hallway corner. She didn't face him only nodded and let her hand fall to the light switch. He scrunched his legs up and laid as comfortably as he could on the makeshift bed. This wasn't going to be an easy sleep.

Daniel dreamt of a red dragon with teeth like spears and breath so putrid it didn't need fire to do him harm. He awoke in a sweat as the great beast bit into his torso. He blinked until his night vision settled. The short love seat had cramped his bladder. He crept to the bathroom to take a piss. He could hear someone snoring in the bedroom. Probably that lout Meg.

He left the door half-open using some light to aim with. He let out a steady stream right in the porcelain bowl that made a huge splash. He corrected his aim to the side to cut down the sound. The trailer wasn't insulated well for heat or sound. He heard Meg and Jayla murmuring earlier tonight before he drifted off to sleep. He dribbled to the end and started to zip up.

"Quite a rod you got there."

He about fell over. Meg stood in the doorway giving his crotch a gander. He pulled his shorts up and could only stand there and blush.

"The guards always wanted to show their wangs to us in the pen. But none of them hold a candle to that rocket you got there, boy howdy."

He finally just pushed past her since she wasn't going to move. She followed him into the living room. He got his blanket and tried to ignore her by curling back up on the painful loveseat. Meg sat on the recliner.

"You and Jayla aren't what they call kissing cousins, are you? I mean this being Kentucky and all."

Daniel threw off his blanket and sat up to face her. "She's my cousin. Best friend I've ever had. The only friend I've ever had. If ..."

"If I hurt her you hurt me?" She stood up. "Sounds like you would kill for her. That's okay in my book. Try not to take all of us down with your next kamikaze routine."

She left him in the living room. He could either fume or sleep. He couldn't do both. He tried Dr. Rhiney's counting breath technique to focus on sleeping. Breath in and out counts as one. He got to ninety-seven and grabbed the TV remote. He channel-surfed till the sun came up.

SEVEN

ALL THREE OF THEM WERE CLIMBING through some thicket a little after ten in the morning. It was cool and the tall trees filled with burnt ochre leaves blocked any warmth from the sun. His hands were on wet fallen leaves as he crouched down with them. Squirrels could be heard climbing in the oak and maple trees. Birds calling to potential mates or rivals.

Jayla handed him some field glasses. "The club charges money for parking over there. We'll have to set up some spikes or nails to stop them from chasing us."

He looked through the binoculars toward the club and then the parking lot. "Won't we be traveling back up the woods to where we parked today?"

"Yeah, but if things go wrong the cops and bettors might come after their money. Don't need a posse on our ass right away." Jayla stood up and brushed off the forest floor's debris from her leggings.

Meg said, "We'll sabotage their ATVs. Leave one for us to haul our take up here where Jayla will be waiting. Then we cruise out of here with a cool million at least. Maybe more."

"We should have more people." He handed Jayla back the field glasses.

Meg cupped her cheeks in frustration. "You want to cut more slices in the pie? I don't even know why you're here."

"He's here because I trust him. And we need him."

Meg shoved up off him to get up from her crouch. "I ain't babysitting no bug-eyed psycho. He either gets up to speed or gets left behind."

He used his right hand to scoop her heel as she stepped. The action swept her to the ground on the wet leaves. She rolled to face him on all fours. He rose with both fists balled up. The coolness of the forest drained off of him. Heat roiled from him.

Jayla slid between them. "Knock it off. Meg, go check on the car. Make sure no one is there."

"Don't send me on errands girlie." But she started up the hill back to the car.

His cousin wiped her brow and then pushed Daniel. "If you two can't get along, we won't be able to pull this off."

"She's the psycho. What are you two to each other?"

"It's complicated." She took out her vape pen, took a drag, and plumed minty vapor.

"You were always a tomboy. I was surprised when you told me about this shitty ex-boyfriend. But Meg? She's not your type at all."

"You don't know what my type is. You've been out of my life for ten years. Don't go telling me what my type is okay?"

He backed up. "You're right. I just want you to be happy. And that loud ass, mean mouth will never make you happy."

"She hasn't hurt me. She's kept me safe."

He rubbed the back of his neck. "She's trouble."

"We're all trouble. Better go before she leaves us in the woods."

She put her arm around his shoulders and led him up the hill. He looked back over the shoulder to the Bluegrass Sportsman Club. How would they ever pull this heist off? They were broken members of an outcast society. They never got what they deserved and he didn't think that would happen anytime soon. Maybe this time they could have some say in their destiny for good or for ill.

Jayla and Meg had some errands to run so they dropped him off at the end of the long gravel driveway to the trailer. It was a crisp fall day but it was bright and sunny. He didn't mind the chance to stretch his legs. As he neared the trailer, he saw a shiny black Dodge Charger parked next to Jayla's old pickup truck. Even the rubber tires had a sheen to them. Vanity plates read QCK CAT.

He slowly stuck his head in the trailer's front door. It was unlocked. He wasn't nervous for some reason. "Hello?"

No one answered so he pressed further in. The lights were off but the shades were open so there was plenty of light in the trailer proper. A long thin man sat in the recliner. Fully reclined with his big black work boots kicked up. He watched something on his smartphone. Daniel could hear a little noise coming from the speaker.

"I said hello."

The thin man was smiling at his phone. He held up one finger halting their interaction momentarily. Daniel stood where he was. He took inventory of the room and potential weapons to use. Knives were in the kitchen too far away. He guessed it was fisticuffs then. The man guffawed at his phone placing it in his shirt pocket.

"What's your name?" the stranger asked with a generous smile.

"Don't you think when you're in someone else's place the proper etiquette is to introduce yourself first." He turned his stance slightly.

Still smiling, the man held up two hands. "Sure, but I know for a fact this ain't your place."

"Maybe I'm the new tenant. Who are you?" Daniel didn't know where this courage was coming from. Yes, he did. From being around his cousin. She was bringing it out of him.

"Maybe I'm a Martian." No more smiles. "Where is Jayla?"

"Who?"

The tall, thin fellow pulled the recliner together and checked Daniel out. He didn't seem impressed. He stood up with a snap and Daniel took a sharp step back. The smile came back.

"Okay, Little Owl. Tell Jayla when she comes back that her friend was looking for her." He went out of the trailer door and down the porch steps. Even though his vanity plate read cat, the man reminded Daniel of a lean greyhound with high hips and long legs. He put on some mirror-lens sunglasses.

Daniel watched him from the open door get into his slick car. Windows tinted past the legal limit. He backed the car around so it was facing out of the drive. He rolled down his driver's side window. A big smile spread like a cut across his face.

"Don't forget to tell her I was here Little Owl."

Daniel leaned against the porch railing. "Okay, Billy."

The smile turned into a sneer and Billy gunned the Charger taking off. Gravel whipped into the trailer's vinyl skirting like birdshot. It was Daniels's turn to smile now. He went back inside to get something cold to drink. All this false badassery made him thirsty as hell. He found one of Meg's Yoo-hoo and shook it up. The chocolate was too cloying but he finished the whole bottle in one gulp.

He slammed the glass bottle a little too hard on the Formica countertop. The small but heavy bottle shattered. Shard flew everywhere. The neck of the bottle had a sharp slice in it and it cut into his hand. He didn't feel it. He knew the adrenaline had to release somewhere. There was always fallout in his previous blow-ups.

He got a broom from beside the fridge. He brought the wastebasket over. He looked for a dustpan but didn't find any. He used Meg's Sports Illustrated 2019 Big Ten Edition magazine as an improvised dustpan to collect the slivers and shards of glass off the floor. He smiled thinking of the face Meg would make when she got home.

<h1 style="text-align:center">EIGHT</h1>

THE GIRLS GOT BACK to the trailer after dark. Daniel had found the channel for New Japan Wrestling and had settled in to watch rerun matches. The masked wrestlers of Japan and Mexico were his favorite. They were smooth and dynamic athletes. Leaping from turnbuckles with kicks or elbows. Spitting in the face of gravity for one shot at glory. He envied their intricate masks.

He wished he could control his body the way they did. He was clumsy or awkward until that moment his rage reached the boiling point. Then it was as if he scooted over to the passenger seat and let someone else drive the car. He was along for the ride but didn't have a hand on the wheel or a foot on the gas. Dr. Rhiney described this as a limited fugue state. Instead of days trapped in one, he was in one for a matter of seconds.

Meg and Jayla laughed their way into the place. The way their strides weaved he knew they had at least been drinking maybe more. Jayla came over to the loveseat. Meg went to the refrigerator and stuck her blockhead in searching. She shuffled some items around.

"I thought I had one more Yoo-hoo in here?"

Jayla looked at Daniel. He mimed a shush with a finger to his lips. She laughed. "We'll pick up a case of the damn things tomorrow hon."

"I was jonesing for one now. Dammit." Meg walked over to the loveseat and saw that wrestling was on TV.

"I thought you didn't like sports?"

"I don't hate sports. But I love wrestling, MMA, boxing, and any of the combat sports."

'Who is your favorite wrestler?" Meg was animated positively for once.

"I like a lot of guys but pushed into a corner. My all-time favorite is Jushin Thunder Liger."

"The Japanese dude with the mask? Man, he's ancient. But you really can't tell how old with that crazy mask on."

"I watch his matches from the eighties on video. His style is wild."

"Who else floats your boat?"

"Ever heard of Mistico?"

Meg shook her head. Jayla yawned but Daniel was on a roll.

"He's a luchador with a silver mask. He was on WWE for a bit but his best work is from the CMLL. Those aren't easy to find matches but there is a forum online that you can check."

"I didn't see any computer at your place," said Jayla.

He said, "I use the library's computer. Order some DVDs to watch at home."

Meg interrupted, "I see a little pattern. You like the masked guys. That makes sense with your effed-up eyes and face."

Jayla said, "Meg! Not cool."

Daniel reached for the sunglasses he had put on the side table. He was caught up in the wrestling and forgot he wasn't wearing them. He placed them back on. Tucked his chin to his chest.

Meg had her arms spread out. "No, I'm on to something. Hear me out."

"I'm begging you," said his cousin.

"Your glasses are like Jushin Liger's mask. They hide you from the audience. From people." She made goggles with her hand and fingers and put them around her eyes.

He said, "I don't know about that."

Meg slapped his leg. "Pretty cool. You can't wear a luchador mask in public but you can slide on those shades anytime you want. Oh, that's the name."

"What?"

"All the masked guys have names. The Spoiler, Dr. X, Rey Misterio, Jr., Mr. Wrestling."

"I don't like where this is heading."

"We'll call you Mr. Shades." She was laughing.

"I don't know. Mr. Shades?"

She countered, "Dr. Shades."

"That's not bad."

Jayla got up in a huff. "I'm glad you two are finally bonding but I'm bored, drunk, and tired. Good night."

Daniel started back in with Meg on his wrestling name then realized he forgot to tell Jayla about Billy stopping by. A wrestler power slammed an opponent on the TV and Meg whooped. He would let his cousin sleep soundly tonight and tell her in the morning.

They were on the road to Bradfordsville for a meet with Kayla's inside man Carl Donger. Daniel sat in the back of the car slouching with his hood way up. He woke up in a black mood after such a good evening watching wrestling. It hit him as the sun poked through the blinds that he was putting his life in the hands of a couple of strangers. There didn't seem any other way to help Jayla.

He wasn't rich. He wasn't particularly smart. Hell, he wasn't even clever. He guessed Meg was right. He was just their resident psycho. Break glass in case of emergency. He didn't have the nerve to ask Jayla if that's how she saw him. Worse he didn't know if he would believe her anyway. Dr. Rhiney said our mind runs with our worst thoughts if we let them. And Daniel was running a track meet at this moment.

They were passing through downtown Lebanon on Main Street. Decorations for Ham Day Festival hung all over town. Signs pronounced the festival was this coming in two weekends. Lots of traffic and visitors in this town in the next couple of weeks. Maybe he would be forgotten in the mix.

"You didn't tell me about the upcoming Ham Festival."

"Nothing to worry about. Just means people will be distracted," said his cousin.

Meg piped, "Yeah, and more people means we can get lost in the cars leaving and going from town."

"I'll leave the scheming in the hands of you, seasoned jailbirds."

He saw a little girl peeking at him when they stopped at the only red light in the city of Lebanon. He gave a slight wave of his fingers. She smiled and waved back as the car pulled away from the light. Meg gunned it a little and they flew out of town a little too fast.

"Easy girl. Don't want to get caught before we meet Carl. He's more skittish than our man in the back."

"Cautious isn't the same thing as skittish."

Jayla leaned over the front seat to face her cousin. "There's risk involved but if we get eighty percent of this job right. We change all of our lives for the better."

"If," he said.

Meg said, "Where is El Shades from last night? Because that guy was cool."

He pulled the drawstrings on his hoodie tight. "The other guy woke up this morning. And he's not understanding this Carl Donger play."

Jayla sighed. "He gets us access to the money room without having to strong-arm our way in. Less violence is better."

He did have to agree with that. While he was quick

to use aggression, the aftermath wasn't worth it. The grief and shame it brought him. Also, the legal problems weighed him down. Fighting only brought him momentary relief so far. Maybe this time it could help Jayla get out of her ex-boyfriend's grasp.

"We're here. Don't spook Carl. He's the key to the whole thing."

Carl wanted their meeting somewhere private. This county had acres and acres of wooded land but everyone knew everybody and their business. Their inside guy was spooked he would be affiliated with Jayla so he kept most contact with a burner cell phone. But for some reason, he wanted a face-to-face today. He had texted his cousin this morning right after Daniel had told her about Billy visiting her trailer the day before.

She used Billy's being there to emphasize the severity of her predicament. Archie could crush her at any time. She had worked herself up into a tizzy then she got the message from Carl to meet up. Which should have made her more nervous but had the opposite effect. He thought he knew how to read Jayla but he supposed a ten-year absence and some bad bounces changed everyone a little.

Carl's idea of privacy was the St. Rose Catholic Church on a Thursday at ten in the morning. Plenty of time after morning mass. And the sinners of Marion County had better things to do than to take their chances hanging around a church in the off-hours. Meg took the car around the back of the tall cathedral-like church. An old Ford pickup truck was parked in the corner under a poplar tree. The leaves are afire in reds and orange.

An older black man puffing on a cigarette sat on the rear of the pickup. There was no tailgate attached anymore. He kicked his legs back and forth as they circled to park. He stubbed out his cig and approached them. Jayla got out trying to reach her contact first. Meg and Daniel slowly got out of the car. Meg stretched and smoothed the pants legs of her jeans.

"Why we meeting Carl? Thought it was best if we had no physical contact. So, no one could put two and two together?"

"This county likes to jabber that's true. You know who else likes to jabber? Billy. He was jabbering to Archie all morning about some weird dude at Jayla's place."

"That don't change our plan. Archie's got his hands full running the championship derby to worry about me and a weird dude."

Carl pointed a finger up. "Now I would expect that is true. But you scratch that little part of his lizard brain Jayla. I don't know why but you cause him consternation."

"Fuck his consternation. I want his money. I want him on his knees. What do you want Carl?"

"I want the Bluegrass Sportsman Club. You know that girl."

"I do. So, what's got you so nervous that we got to meet in person?"

Carl said, "Billy has orders to up the game on you now. Archie said and I quote. Take it to the limit."

Daniel asked, "That some kind of warning?"

"Kid, Archie don't warn. He just acts. She knows what I mean."

Jayla circled away and came back. "Means they will sick the KFM's trained law dogs on me. Get me locked up for good."

"It was a good play, girl but you have to get out of town. And pronto."

Jayla's voice was laced with steel. "I'm not going anywhere until I get that money."

Carl took out another cigarette, flicked open his Zippo, and lit up. After he blew a plume of smoke up, he said, "I knew you were too crazy to quit. But you have to lay low until Saturday. Get out of that trailer and find some other place to hide until the mains."

Jayla folded her arms. Her vape pen was in her right hand and she took a quick pull. She spoke around the escaping vape tendrils. "Who's working security Saturday night then? Staties?"

Carl nodded. "Those are some tough hombres. Still feeling froggy enough to make your play?"

Meg said, "Ain't no thing but a chicken wing."

Carl smiled. "I'm not risking much. Bump on my head from you all to make my wounded pride look real. You guys could get your asses shot off. Then they go to work on you."

"I reckon that would scare most people off but I'm a walking corpse right now anyway. As long as Archie has his power with Johnny Mudd and the KFM."

Daniel said, "You know there is another option. Come to Louisville. Hell, move to Chicago. Or the Moon. Just leave."

"Not that simple. I can't just take off."

He came up close to her. "I didn't hear no reason why not."

She unfolded her arms and shoved him away. "I just can't! Leave it be Daniel."

Carl shook his head. "Find somewhere else to go for a couple of days. Don't go back home to your trailer. Leave the area soon as we're done."

Meg, "All my Yoo-hoo is back there."

Carl pointed a crooked finger at her. "Maybe you all have your heads too far up your asses to pull this off."

Jayla said, "No, no. We got this. Just wound a little tight, man. Thanks for the warning. We'll scat. Next time you see us will be Saturday night at the back door."

She held out her fist for a bump. The old black man gave her a firm hug instead. She accepted the embrace laying her head on his shoulder. Daniel wondered what that was about. After the hug, Carl got in his old farm truck and they watched him pull away. Rock dust kicked up in his trail.

"Old man's a worrywart," said Meg.

"Don't make light of him."

Daniel asked, "Where we going to go until Saturday?"

Jayla went over to the passenger side. "Not too far but far enough. Lebanon Junction maybe?"

Meg opened her driver's side door. "You asking or telling?"

Jayla looked over the roof. "Telling. We have all the gear for the job in the trunk. We leave for LJ now."

She and Meg got in the car. Daniel still leaned on the

wheel well. Meg pounded the outside of her door with the flat of her palm. "Giddy up Shades."

He pulled his hood up and got in the car with his accomplices. That's what they would be charged with. He would ride the full rap. Could feel it in his bones. Aching. He didn't have any of his pills on him.

Jayla turned to face him. "What's eating you?"

"All my underwear is back at the trailer."

"You've never lived in the same drawers for a few days? It will be like camping."

"I've never been camping with girls."

Meg hooted. "Then you've been missing out."

She peeled out kicking gravel all over the poplar tree they had parked next to. As they turned the corner around St. Rose, Meg flipped the holy building the bird. And that bird wasn't a dove. Wasn't a dove at all.

NINE

THE ROUTE TO LEBANON JUNCTION had a couple of routes but both took them back through Lebanon. They could go through Springfield or head around the other way through Raywick and New Haven. Both ways bypassed Loretto staying clear of Jayla's trailer. His cousin said to take the New Haven path so they could stop at Missy's Out of the Way Café. It was just outside of Raywick and Jayla said their steak was the best. Daniel didn't have an appetite.

The one-level café was built from pine wood that the sun had turned gray. Small lights hung from the edge of the roof. Wire decorative chairs on the deck for people to sit outside. He passed a statue of a cobra its hood up as they walked into the café. He wished it was real and would sink its fangs into him. Get the venom in deep and end his charade of a life.

Dr. Rhiney would say inner thoughts are reflected in outer actions. Jayla observed the darkening of his mood. She tried to get him to relax by joking and making light of their past. Meg laughed not unlike the baboons he cleaned up after at the zoo. His cousin had her work cut out for her. It wasn't wise to have him mix with people right now.

"Welcome to Missy's. Just be the three of you?" The waitress had on jeans and her long bright blond hair up in a ponytail.

Jayla said, "Yes ma'am. And can we get a table by the window please?"

"Surely can."

The waitress led them through the café that had memorabilia and old signs plastered on the ceiling and walls. Strings of beads, streamers, flags, balloons, and even a baseball bat hung down from the ceiling like a stalactite in a cave. The dining tables and chairs were varied but all light wood. She brought them to a table that sat five by the window and laid out the menus.

"Sweet tea for everybody?"

Daniel said, "Water for me."

"Gotcha hon." And the waitress was off.

Meg looked around. "Ain't very crowded for being so good."

"It's 11:20 on a Thursday. You should see it on the

weekends. Joint is jumping. You would be sitting outside by that stone cobra."

Meg didn't even look at the menu. "I'll get the steak like you said."

"There are other steaks but the specialty is the Nicole. It comes with these thin crispy fries. You'll love them."

Over his menu, Daniel watched Jayla pat Meg's hand on the table. He folded his menu up and placed it on the table. He looked left, right then centered his gaze on his cousin. She attempted to read his thoughts but failed.

"You getting the steak Daniel?"

"I'm not hungry."

"At least get the fries. You don't eat them now you can take them for later."

Daniel popped his knuckles. "What's going on?"

Jayla scrunched up her face. "We're fixing to eat some good steak."

He pointed back and forth between the two women at the table. "How long have you two been a couple?"

Meg showed a lot of teeth in her smile. Jayla was more nervous but she said, "Long enough."

"You tell me you had a thing with Archie. Which threw me off because I didn't expect that from an avowed tomboy like yourself. Now it looks like you two have the hots for each other. Makes more sense to me but I'm in the dark a little."

Jayla bent forward and spoke in a quiet voice. "Yes, me and Meg are together now. She's a lesbian. I like men and women. Nobody cares what we do as long as we don't advertise. So, keep your damn voice down capeesh?"

He bent forward. "Just don't act like I'm some hick from the holler."

"Oh, that's right you're from the big city. All sophisticated with your Pride Parades and such." She got out her vape pen and took a pull.

The waitress came back with two sweat teas and a glass of water for Daniel. She gauged the temperature of the table pretty quickly. She gave the brightest smile and took out her order book.

"Have you all decided what you want or do you need some more time?"

Meg said, "Two Nicoles and the sourpuss will have a hissy fit then go sit in the car."

The waitress's eyes got wide. "I see. Well, sugar if you decide you want something later just flag me down. I'll get your steaks going."

Jayla said, "That ain't helping Meg."

She said, "I'm tired of tiptoeing around him. Like he's a bomb waiting to go off. If he can't handle the pressure in a café, he sure can't handle it Saturday night."

Daniel drank from his glass overflowing with ice. The cold water couldn't fight back the heat flushing through his body. He switched to his breathing technique. That worked a little. Chasing his breath in and out. He had inadvertently closed his eyes. When he opened them, Meg was smirking and Jayla frowning.

"Do we need to go?" asked his cousin.

"I'm doing the job. You all need me. I'm under control."

Meg mocked him with a robotic voice. "I am under control."

Jayla elbowed her hard. "You're the oldest person at this table. Why don't you act like it?"

"I'll do whatever the hell I want."

They started to argue and Daniel stayed out of it. He reached a calmness with his breathing. The first time it sunk in so deep. Could he be getting better? He would bring this up at his next session with Dr. Rhiney with a few details left out. He was starting to feel a little hungry when he looked past his cousin and Meg out the window into the parking lot where a county deputy had pulled his cruiser into.

He tried to get their attention. "Cop."

They kept flapping their gums. He shook his finger out the window. "Hey guys, cop."

They still were too intent on stoking their argument to hear his warning. He grabbed both their arms from across the table and squeezed.

"Ow, godammit. What did you pinch me for?"

"A cop just pulled up."

Jayla hooded her face with her hands. "Is he in here yet?"

Daniel had a perfect view of him. "No, he's too busy checking out our ride."

Meg whipped around to look. "Damn, he sure is. Girl, we got all our stuff in the trunk."

Daniel assumed that was the guns and whatever tools they needed for the job Saturday night. His cousin sneaked a look outside. She quickly turned back around to face away from the window. She went a little pale.

"Shit. That's Larry. He's worked one of Archie's matches before."

Meg said, "He wouldn't recognize you after one time, would he?"

"He's seen me around time for other stuff I'm sure. Are the plates good?"

"Yeah, the plates are legal for the car." Meg seemed cool as a cucumber.

Daniel watched the deputy circle the car. He inspected the tires and pursed his lips. Big mirrored sunglasses guarded his eyes. He was a barrel-chested man who wore his hair burr short. Jayla got up and looked around.

"I'm going to go hide in the bathroom for a minute. Maybe slip out the back if there is a back. Hide in some bushes or something till he is gone."

Meg, "I think you're being silly."

Jayla was already in the hallway where the bathrooms were. A bell dinged and in walked the deputy. He removed his glasses and hung them in his shirt pocket. The waitress spoke to him and the big deputy let out a hearty laugh. She touched his shoulder three times in their brief conversation. She handed him a white bag and a Styrofoam cup of what was probably coffee. He was picking up a to-go order.

Meg smiled at him. "See nothing to worry about."

Daniel still had his calm on tap. He watched the waitress playfully touch the deputy's large bicep. He laughed again and said something to her. The waitress got a puzzled look on her face and then pointed to their table. Daniel's pulse jumped.

"He's coming over."

Meg said, "Stay frosty kid."

She took a long drink of her sweet tea and sat the glass down right as the deputy arrived at the table. He gave that shit-eating grin only law enforcement can. Daniel balled his fists under the table.

"Tammy said that's your all's Ford Fusion Sport out there?"

Meg said, "She's a beaut."

The deputy said, "Does it really do 130?"

Meg winked at the deputy. "Well, I heard it can but I've never had the pleasure."

The deputy laughed. "I'm sure you haven't, Miss. I was thinking about getting one but wasn't sure if I would like it. I'm a classic muscle car fiend."

Meg nodded. "For sure. I'm a big gearhead but I couldn't pass up this deal. Got it from my grandmother who didn't realize what kind of beast was under the hood."

Daniel couldn't believe his eyes. She was charming. He chanced a look towards the restrooms but didn't see his cousin. He saw the waitress and she looked a little jealous. If only she knew Meg.

The deputy tipped his coffee cup in a mock toast. "You've given me something to consider. Enjoy your lunch."

The deputy left their table for the door. He said some words to the waitress and she brightened back off. He was out in the gravel parking lot and into his police cruiser. Marion County Deputy emblazoned on the side panels. Daniel watched the deputy's every movement. Meg watched Daniel's face.

She said, "Little piggy gone?"

"You mean the big piggy with the gun? Yes, your new best friend has left." He took a drink of his water.

"You peed a little didn't you?"

He choked on the water coughing out a response. "Almost. I thought cops could sniff out ex-cons."

"Some can. Deputy Doo-right there couldn't. We got lucky."

Their waitress brought over two plates of steaming hot steaks with a side pile of shoestring fries. Meg got her plate placed in front of her and the waitress sat down Jayla's order.

"Enjoy. Your friend in the bathroom?"

Meg said, "She had to leave for an emergency."

"Oh, sorry to hear that. Would you like me to box up her meal?"

"No, I think my friend here has his appetite back. He'll eat it. But can you all make another one to go? I'll take it to her later."

"Sure, thing hon." And the waitress scooted off to place that order.

"We going to let Jayla hide out in the bushes?"

Meg sliced off a piece of the peppery steak. "Damn skippy. She was being a bitch earlier before the fuzz got here. Let her stew a little bit."

He stammered, "I don't know if I can do that."

She slid Jayla's plate over to him. "Try this steak. It is delish."

She was right about his hunger coming back. Once that adrenaline started to settle his appetite returned. He cut off a piece and took a bite. It was buttery soft. Heaven in his mouth.

She said, "Dip it in their house sauce."

He did as she asked with the next piece he cut off. After one bite, Daniel said, "Let her stew."

TEN

JAYLA COLD-SHOULDERED THEM all the way to Lebanon Junction after they picked the bramble from her hair. She did eat her steak in the car against Meg's protest. Jayla had told her once she was done, she was going to wipe her face down the dashboard if she felt like it. When he put his hand on her shoulder to apologize, she stuck it with her fork. This was hornet-level mad.

His cousin had a huge well of emotions. She could be the happiest person in the state of Kentucky or the most furious person you would ever meet. And they were not random emotional outbursts. Her emotions were always appropriate when they occurred. She just threw her whole self into every moment. The very thought exhausted Daniel.

He had been down every winding country road he could imagine in the last couple of days. Crowded woods opened to browning pastures on never-ending narrow asphalt lanes. He could never find his way home now without help from a local or GPS. The two-lane road they were on merged into one lane. That's when he knew he left civilization behind.

It was a gray September day. Meg had called it an Ohio-type of sky. They drove on this one lane for a few miles never encountering any other vehicle. Houses either sat close to the road or so far back past the trees they couldn't see them. A yellow mutt barked and gave chase around one bend in the road. The dog finally gave up and went back.

Jayla pointed to a large pewter mailbox up on the right. "We're here."

"Where is here?" He noticed the mailbox was faux distressed. Artsy rustic.

"103 Winding Hollow Rd. Aunt Kelly's place."

"That's insane. We were actually on a road called Winding Hollow?"

"LJ isn't known for subtlety."

Meg took the right into the gravel driveway. A large, old barn with a hayloft was on their left. The wood slats were gray from the sun and the other elements but it was built to last. There was some wire fencing that ran around the length of a field they passed. They climbed a slight incline towards a modern two-story house with a three-car garage that sat at the top of the hill.

They parked their car in front of the garage. When they shut the car doors, he thought they sounded extremely loud in the quiet countryside. The beautiful stone house nestled right up to an old-growth forest. Someone in his family had money after all.

"Aunt Kelly owns this place?"

Jayla said, "Yeah. Her and that slick husband of hers. Jonathan works out of Louisville. Surprised you two ain't met."

"I don't believe our paths have crossed. Where's Johnny work at?"

"Some money management shell game bullshit. And it's Jonathan, never call him Johnny." She traipsed up the large blood-red front door.

"I'll make sure not to do that when we're inside."

She fished in her pocket. "Oh, they aren't here. On vacation in Italy, I think. Out of the country anyways."

He grabbed her sleeve. "Tell me we aren't busting into their house?"

She tugged her sleeve away. "Relax, I got a key."

And she had a key when she pulled her hand from her pocket. She stuck it in the lock and it opened for her. Jayla put her hand on the doorknob but halted opening it. She looked at him and Meg.

"There is an alarm code I have to enter on a security keypad. I think I remember it but in case I don't be ready to hotfoot it to the car."

He said, "I thought Aunt Kelly gave you the key?"

"I said I had a key."

"You stole a key? So, we are breaking onto her house."

"Is it really breaking in when you have a key? You are so literal I swear. Now, wait out here." She opened the door and dashed in before he could protest more.

Meg said, "We don't have a key for the Bluegrass Sportsman Club. You going to whine about that too?"

Daniel ignored her and looked off the concrete porch. No one was watching but he still felt eyes upon him. He could always feel it when he was being observed. Judged and weighed Dr. Rhiney would say. She would also tell him it was his perception that mattered not other people's. He still wasn't there yet but he was trying.

He felt a hand on his shoulder and flinched. Meg arched an eyebrow.

"She yelled it's safe to come in. You see someone?"

He stepped out of his head and through the door. "Don't think so. Just felt something."

She followed him into the two-story foyer. A grand staircase with dark cherry steps and handrails dominated the interior. The walls were white and the ceilings high. A decorative modern chandelier made of polished brass hung from the ceiling. Aunt Kelly had bank.

"One of the Durand family found a way to the top. Maybe I should marry a rich guy," said Jayla coming out of a hallway carrying a glass with some purple drink in it.

"Or you could knock off the super bowl of cockfighting," said Meg.

"Marry or steal. Those are the keys to wealth and riches." She took a big gulp of her purple drink. "Ah. Help yourselves to the soda machine in the kitchen. Mi casa es su casa."

Meg laughed and went past her into the kitchen. She slapped Jayla's butt on her way by. He walked over to his cousin. She offered him her glass but he waved her off. They both took in the scope and scale of the house. A large painting of impressionistic art hung on one wall. A clay vase the color of red clay rested on a beautiful teak table.

"Do you know anyone in our family with taste and money?"

She answered, "Those are two traits none of us possess."

"Aunt Kelly will murder us if she finds out, won't she?"

"She certainly does possess that Durand family trait. Let's make sure she never finds out."

Daniel pressed his fingers into his forehead. "She probably has us on video already."

"We'll erase the footage."

"I don't have a computer or a fancy phone like you but doesn't that stuff goes to the cloud now."

"Quit worrying. Meg knows some sneaky thief shit. She'll figure something out."

He checked his cousin out. She wasn't worried in the least bit. "Dammit. Aunt Kelly gave you that key. She doesn't care if you're here."

She looped an arm around his shoulder. "That's right, kid. I'm her favorite. She told me I could stay here if I wanted any time."

He said, "Then why all the theatrics?"

She drained her drink and handed him her glass.

"Because you all took your sweet time eating steaks while I sat hunched on a wet spot in the bushes. Now fetch me another grape soda."

He took her glass and went towards the kitchen where he heard Meg making a ruckus. "That's another family trait you know."

She said, "What's that?"

"Holding grudges."

"Wait," she said.

He put his hand on the wall before he entered the kitchen. Something in her voice gave him concern. She sat down on the second to last step of the stairwell. He walked back over and leaned on the railing by her. She got out her vape pen and huffed out a big ball of mint vapor. She sheepishly looked up.

"Aunt Kelly would kill me if she saw me doing that in here."

He said, "You come here a lot?"

She shrugged. "I would stop by from time to time. She liked to hear about my crazy life. We would have a drink or two and chat. I think she was lonely."

"Her husband gone a lot?"

"Yeah, but I think he loves her. Genuinely. But his work is how they afford this place and the trips they take. So, she was lonely. After my tall tales, she would tell me some whoppers of hers. From the wild old days." She smiled.

"Aunt Kelly was wild? My Mom yeah but Aunt Kelly?"

"As a buck. She was the middle child of twelve kids. Would you know which kid was home and which was out all night? I wouldn't. She and I were cut from the same cloth." She sucked on the vape pen again.

"When I took up with Archie, I didn't come around as much. After he started hitting on me, I stopped coming by at all. Eventually, Aunt Kelly came knocking on my door. She saw me all worn out and ragged. She suspected something but didn't outright ask me."

Daniel kept quiet but moved onto the step next to her. Not holding her just sitting so close their hips and legs connected.

"That last time he put me in the ER. The one I told you about. Afterward, I came here. Aunt Kelly let me stay here with no bullshit questions. She gave me comfort and helped my body heal."

He bumped her knee. "She sounds pretty cool."

"She was there for me. Didn't call my Mom. Just…she was just present. Like she soaked up my pain and fear from me. I owe her a lot." She took a pull and let the vape cloud release up her cheeks.

Daniel waved the vapor from between them. "We can call this thing off."

She sat up straight. "What the hell are you talking about? Call off the job?"

"I thought you were all alone but sounds like Aunt Kelly is there for you."

"Are you wussing out? You are, aren't you? Don't do this to me. Not now. I need you."

"Why can't you just move away? Or get an attorney to fight the harassment? There are other options besides stealing from your mobbed-up ex."

She stood up, faced him, and shouted, "He took something from me. And I'm taking it back."

She went to the front door and flung it wide open. "If you want to leave, get to stepping."

Meg came out of the kitchen with a gigantic stacked sandwich. Mayonnaise dotted the corner of her mouth. "What's all the yelling about?"

"Daniel's a big pussy and was quitting on us." His cousin pointed her finger out the door as she stared him down.

"Cool," Meg said. She took a big bite of her sandwich and retreated into the kitchen.

He got up and slammed the door shut. "Drama queen. I never said I was quitting. When is it a crime to ask questions?"

They faced each other. Jayla was taller than the average woman. Daniel was of average height for a man. She poked him in the chest. "You're in or out. No conditions or clauses. In or out. That's all I want to hear out of your mouth."

He went to speak and she held a finger up in his face. "Think before you utter a word."

He pushed her finger out of his face. "In."

ELEVEN

"YOU'RE HOLDING IT TOO TIGHT," said Meg.

She stood behind him coaching him how to shoot the pistol. They were behind the house in the woods. Aunt Kelly's husband Jonathan had cleared out space as his improvised gun range. Busted two-liter soda bottles were hanging by a string from the bottom of a five-foot wooden frame. On the top shelf of the frame were beer bottles and cans lined up.

"If I don't hold it tight, the damn thing will jump out of my hand."

"Right but if you squeeze it too tight you shake and throw the aim off. Here let's try it with some help."

She came up close behind him and lined her arms

along his outstretched arms. Her hands cupped his. Her touch was light but also firm. So close her breath on his neck gave him goosebumps. She must have felt them along his arm. She spoke calmly and quietly in his ear, "Easy. Just like this. Loose but steady. Okay now, aim at the Pabst Blue Ribbon can."

He centered the gun's sight on the can. She corrected a little more. He felt her set her hips into his buttocks anticipating the recoil. He couldn't help but get aroused a little from the close and tender contact with the taller woman. And she smelled good too.

She said softly, "Fire."

A loud tock of the pistol then a ping from the can as it flipped off the frame. He did it. One shot and he finally hit the target.

"I see what you're saying, Meg. Don't be so tight and rigid. Just stay loose, squeeze, and let it go." He pointed the gun down range but was turning it in his hand inspecting his grip.

She was still close to his body but had her two hands on his shoulders when she said, "Yeah, it's like fucking. You don't want to be too tight and blow your wad too soon."

Daniel's surprise caused him to pull the trigger and fire the gun. The recoil punched his elbow into his face knocking his glasses akimbo. He dropped the gun and fixed his glasses. His face blushed red as a beet.

Meg roared with laughter. "Just like that. Oh my god, that was priceless."

She picked up the gun and brushed off some pine needles. She checked the slide to make sure it was good.

Satisfied she made eye contact with the embarrassed Daniel, brought the barrel close to her mouth, gave a pouty look, and blew on the barrel.

"You aren't going to tell Jayla, are you?"

"That you're a premature ejaculator? I wish I didn't know."

"Knock it off."

"I'd be more embarrassed about my poor shooting skills if I were you."

She took a wide stance, stuck the pistol out at the targets, and fired three times. A water bottle exploded, a brown beer bottle shattered and another can flipped off the frame. Pretty impressive he had to say. He doubted he would ever be that proficient.

"Popping cans is easy. When the blood is pounding in your ears and your vision goes narrow, you just need to empty your clip into the person shooting at you. Everyone misses. Even up close."

She watched his face and said, "What?"

"I know that feeling. Adrenaline."

"Yeah, most folk can't handle the surge."

Daniel didn't say that's the place he felt most at home. A duck in water.

"You don't think there will be shooting anyway at the club?"

"I would love to shoot Archie but no. With Carl getting us in we bypass all the guards. Might need to point your guns at some people but doubt you'll need to fire."

"Fine with that. I hope I don't have to pull any trigger."

"Just follow mine and Jayla's lead." She pointed the gun down range again checking the site.

He had taken off his hooded zip-up sweatshirt when they had started shooting. For some reason under the shaded trees, he got hot. Now the sweat on his arms and the small of his back chilled him. He got his black hoodie off the ground by a pine tree, put it on, and zipped it up to his chin careful not to catch his beard. He couldn't believe it was Friday.

Tomorrow night he would be holding up a damn cock-fighting club. When his teacher at St. Bernard's passed out the Campbells Test that showed what career you were suited for, he got a truck driver. Others got a fireman or teacher. He didn't recall one cockfighting thief. The nuns would be so proud of him.

She said, "You want to stay out here and shoot some more Tex?"

"No, I don't think more of your hands-on instruction would help."

She thwacked him on his back. "Ha. You got a mouth on you. That's probably why you get in so many scraps."

"People tell me right to my face I'm ugly. Every day of my life I hear that at least once. Makes me mean. Makes me want to hurt someone."

She backpedaled towards the house. "You ain't ugly. Ugly is an attitude. Believe me, I've been in foster care. I've seen ugly. Let's go get some grub."

He jabbed his hands in his hoodie pockets. "Jayla's already burned half the pantry."

"She is an awful cook but she's no quitter. Why I love her."

He chuckled. "When we were younger, all the cousins dared each other to jump from one side of the hayloft across a wide gap to the other. Only the older kids could make it but not easy. Jayla kept jumping and missing the edge. Fell twelve feet every time."

"Jesus, she's lucky she didn't break her neck."

"There were some soft spots of clumped hay down below. There was also a ladder and a hardwood floor. But she kept jumping. Everyone got bored and left. She kept jumping. It got dark. She kept jumping. My Mom yelled so I left. Jayla kept jumping."

Meg beamed. "That's my girl."

"Grandma found her the next day laying on the barn floor in a sweaty sleep. When she scooped her up, Grandma said her arm hung funny. The doctors said she dislocated her shoulder in the night trying to make the leap."

"That's some spirit."

He shook his head. "I had to nearly tackle her the next evening to keep her from trying again. Had her damn arm in a sling and still, she almost got by me. I have to help her Meg. I don't want to do this job but she won't stop till she gets the money or dies trying."

"Ain't nobody dying."

"Sell that to the gun in your hand."

The house was built to let in a lot of natural light. When

it was night though with all the exposed windows and no blinds, Daniel felt exposed. He couldn't peer through the black of the night but anyone could see them in this opulent house. The interior lights would be visible from the winding road and the half-ring thicket behind them. Just raccoons, opossums, and an occasional owl watching, he told himself. Not Archie, Billy, or some other Kentucky Fried Mafia henchman.

He laughed at his paranoia but still couldn't shake the fishbowl feeling. He waited for a giant finger to tap on the glass and shake his whole world apart. Breathe out the bad thoughts. Breathe in positivity. Count his breaths. Find his inner calm. But the clicking of a writing pen interrupted his counting breaths at five.

"And then we corral Beth and Pam into the closet. You'll have to do the talking because they would recognize my voice." She had a pen she clicked in her right hand and her ever-present vape pen in her left grip.

On Aunt Kelly's kitchen table, his cousin had spread some drawing paper and sketched out a layout of the Bluegrass Sports Club. She even cut out little paper dolls representing their heist gang and the guards. With Carl's assistance, they shouldn't come into conflict except for one guard. He and Jayla would wear ski masks. They would both have sidearms.

"We get the loot into our duffel bags. Slip back out the way we came in and use the only working ATV to get us up the hill where Meg is waiting."

"What if someone sees us sabotaging the other four-wheelers?" he asked.

"You have what if-ed me for the last time. This whole goddamn operation is what if."

"Alright. Everything works out how you predict. It won't but let's say it does. We leave. No one shoots at us. What then?"

"We take you back to Louisville. Give you your cut. And you live happily ever after."

"What about you?"

"Meg and I would hang out in the city for a bit. Make sure Archie's business partners kick his ass to the curb before we head back." She pulled on the vape pen and exhaled a minty cloud.

"Why go back at all? Thought you would go to Canada."

"Vancouver. And we will. I just need to pick up some stuff in Loretto first."

"Like what?"

She swept her vape pen as if she was erasing his concerns. "Don't worry about what I have to pick up. It's personal."

"Personal. Why don't we get it now? That way you two can take off once you drop me off. Seems safer to me."

She tried to laugh him off. "Who's the brains of this operation?"

He spun on his bar stool. "I don't think anyone of us has a right to say we're the brains. We might be the Brainless Gang."

She kicked her foot up on the stool halting his spin. "This has to work."

He nodded. "It's a solid enough plan."

"Then what's all the bitching about?"

"In all the shows I've seen, it's the getting away that's the problem."

"We aren't robbing a bank. We're robbing bad guys. They can't go to the law."

"We can't either."

She placed her writing pen and her vape pen next to the map on the table. She got the two paper figures that were supposed to be them. The paper dolls danced around the map. Deftly avoiding the guards, up the hill to the salt shaker where Meg's paper avatar waited in the getaway car. All assembled in the car, Jayla drove it off the table into the air.

"Just that simple?"

"Keeping it simple since 1995."

He took the paper car from her and went to the stove. Clicking a button, a blue flame danced on a front burner. He lit the paper car on fire and let it burn away in his hand. The burnt edges floated to the ground. His cousin stamped them out.

"Clean up your mess. I'm going to call and see what's taking Meg so long with the pizza."

She left the kitchen and he got a paper towel from a roll on the counter. He wet it a little under the faucet. He used the damp paper towel to wipe up the black ash off Aunt Kelly's cream-tiled floor. He had never appreciated a kitchen floor before. Most of the ones he remembered were linoleum or some other cheap laminate. The phrase 'you could eat off this floor' was appropriate.

His cousin came back into the room speaking on her

phone. Her eyes were wide and her voice loud. "I said I'll be there."

She stuck the phone in her pocket and went towards the mudroom on the side of the kitchen. This room was connected to the garage. He followed after Jayla. She moved quickly to the key rack and searched through each key chain. She mumbled to herself. He touched her shoulder and she jumped as if a lightning bolt struck her.

She tapped her fingers to her temple. "He has her."

"Who has who? Meg?"

She nodded. "Archie has her."

"How did that happen?"

"I don't fucking know. He has her and says he'll let her go but he wants to talk with me first."

"Sounds like a trap."

"You think?" She turned back to the key rack hunting for the right one. Her hand fell on a sleek fob and she unhooked it from the rack.

He put his hands on her shoulder, turned her to face him, and took the key fob from her. He looked her in the eyes and said, "A trap."

She slapped him and started bawling. That out-of-control sobbing that reached into your very bones. She covered her face with her hands and shook. Daniel pulled her into a snug embrace. Slowly her shivering came to a stop. He pulled a folded square of paper towels out of his hoodie pocket and offered it to his cousin. She dried her eyes and then blew a big honk into the towel.

"We have to go to the Club. Archie has Meg there. It's

some kind of a trap or a power trip. I don't know but we have to get Meg back." Her voice didn't tremble.

"I'll drive." He went to the garage door and opened it. A light automatically came on illuminating the three-bay garage. The far bay was empty. A burgundy Jaguar SUV sat in the center bay. A sleek black luxury sedan rested in the bay closest to the door.

She came up and stood next to him. "It's Aunt Kelly's new Tesla S."

He held out the key fob to her. "Okay, you drive."

She snatched the keys and hustled to the car. Daniel hoped Aunt Kelly had a lot of insurance.

TWELVE

THEY PULLED UP INTO the big gravel lot of the Bluegrass Sports Club. The lot was dark but as they came closer to the building it was illuminated by strong flood lights on the corners of the roof. Two big Ford pickup trucks, a GMC Yukon SUV, and a car Daniel had seen before were parked close to the entrance. Jayla backed the Tesla into a parking spot close to Billy's Dodge Charger. She faced the nose out for a quick exit.

"You stay here. Have the car ready to roll when I bring Meg out."

He shook his head. "What if you don't come out?"

"He's not going to kill us. He just wants to terrorize me. If I'm dead, that's no fun for him."

He opened his door. "Now I'm really not staying."

She grabbed a handful of his hoodie. "I need calm right now."

He looked into her eyes and saw it. "You think I'll explode in there? Pressure gets too high and I start swinging. That it?"

"I trust you Daniel but these guys don't swing punches. They shoot bullets."

"I'm doing better. I'll keep my cool."

She let go of his sleeve. "I can't worry about you while I'm dealing with Archie."

He crossed his heart. "I swear on my life as a member of the Space Cowboy Cadets. I will be cool."

She laughed. "We ain't been Space Cowboy Cadets since 1997."

"Just keeping it light. I'm cool as a cucumber."

She patted him on the shoulder. "Okay. You're going in but leave the gun in the car."

He placed his pistol under the seat. "Don't they have guns?"

She got out of the car. "Yeah, but Archie will think it's rude if we bring any ourselves."

They approached a double-door entrance covered by a blue awning. He spotted the video camera above them right away. Jayla tried the door but it was locked. She turned to the camera and gave it the finger. A buzz sounded. There was a click at the door and she twisted the knob opening the right door. Into the trap, they went.

He followed his cousin who knew exactly where she was going. The interior was dimly lit. The walls were painted white. Some University of Kentucky sports mostly basketball posters were framed and hung on the wall. The floor was a short nap carpet in a blue and white checker pattern. There was a pleasant fresh odor. The place had been recently cleaned.

They passed a ticket booth like they had at high school gymnasiums. He assumed past the doors beside it was the cockfighting arena. She led them left down a short corridor to the rear of the building. She halted for a moment and pointed back from where they came.

She whispered. "Back past the ticket booth. That's the collection room."

He nodded. She turned and walked to the last door on the left. This door was bright blue. Daniel had seen three cameras so far and took note of the one in the corner behind him. His cousin knocked sharply. The door was opened by a giant with a burr cut. The giant had a brow that a Neanderthal would be proud of.

The doorman moved out of the way so they could enter. It was a large office space that almost felt like someone's den except for the massive oak desk. Slim Billy leaned his ass on one corner of the desk with his arms crossed looking as nonchalant as he could. A man behind the desk balanced a toddler on his knee. He cooed at the little boy paying little attention to him and Jayla.

The rest of the expansive office resembled a lounge with a long leather couch along the wall. A dark wood coffee table was in front of it. Another swollen-up tick of a man sat on one end of the couch with a big automatic pistol on his lap. He had that aggressive quality that painted him as a lawbreaker or law enforcer. A young blond woman in tight low-cut jeans and a revealing spaghetti-string tank top was at the other end of the couch sliding screens on her smartphone.

The man behind the desk said, "Nice night."

Jayla had lip lock. She seemed so tight she vibrated. Daniel swore he could hear a hum as if a tuning fork stood next to him. This must be Archie. Her ex-boy-friend only had eyes for Jayla now. He held the boy up with outstretched hands to his left.

"Ellie, take little Tommy back in the other room please."

The dishwater blond got up from the leather couch along the wall. She gathered young Tommy into her arms looking nervously at his cousin as she left via a side door. Billy moved off his corner of the desk and took the woman's spot on the couch.

Archie said, "Is this the tweaker Billy saw at your place the other day?"

Daniel noticed a tear coming down his cousin's cheek. She looked over her shoulder to check on the man-moun-tain behind them then she took a shot across the room and dove over the desk. Archie's good never had time to grab her. Daniel managed to get in the giant's way behind him. Slowed him down at least. Jayla disappeared behind the desk with the man.

One underling shot off the couch coming to his boss's aid. Billy just smiled and slowly stood up. Suddenly he heard a thick laugh coming from the desk area. Her ex stood up controlling Jayla with a tight hug. It wasn't easy as she twisted and swung her head back trying to connect. The man shoved her towards Billy and the other guy. They held her fast while Archie made a show of dusting himself off.

He bent over and picked up a tumbler that Jayla had knocked off his desk. "You are one wild kitty. I'll tell you what."

She worked up some phlegm. Daniel waited for the spit to fly but the short man held up a finger. "You do that and nice Archie will leave the room."

She swallowed it down. Archie smiled and gave his men the sign to let her go. They stepped back but only a step. Archie said, "Running around with lesbos and tweakers. My how you've changed Jayla."

"Being locked up for six months changes a gal."

"Still sore about that, huh? I gave you options. Chose the wrong one is all."

"Being a punching bag wasn't high on my list."

Archie reached out to brush her cheek. "You're too pretty to be so ugly."

His cousin swatted his hand away. Daniel felt himself leaning on his toes. The flush rose to his neck. Ready to pop. Archie lined him up in his sights. The short man had hunter DNA in him. Daniel reckoned all men did.

"Speaking of ugly." He looked Daniel up left then right. "You ain't fooling no one tweaker. Hiding behind those frames and hoodie."

Daniel said, "Not trying to fool."

"Fooling yourself. Who cares if you're ugly? Own it I say."

Jayla spat, "He ain't ugly."

Archie peered down his nose at her. Pretty hard to do when you are shorter than everyone else. "No? Let's see then. Pull down that hood and take off them glasses tweaker."

Daniel pursed his lips. He let out a breath, pull down his hood, and took off his glasses."

Big howl from Archie. His cackle of hyenas joined their bosses laughing.

"You're one ugly tweaker."

Daniel tamped down the furnace inside. He felt pride in keeping his cool. A month, maybe two weeks ago he would have raged-dance across this whole room. Assholes and elbows till no one was left standing. His cousin might not be safe either. Dr. Rhiney's therapy had paid off.

"I knew you were fugly but Jesus. You should slap your Mom for not aborting you."

Jayla said, "Where's Meg?"

"All business huh girl? Joseph. Go get the dyke."

Joseph was the name of the mountain. He went to the same door that the trashy woman and the little boy left through. He dipped his head under the door frame disappearing into the next room. A few seconds later a beaten Meg stood shakily in the door. She was gagged and her wrists bound by zip tie cuffs. The big man holding her up lest she fell.

"Meg!" Jayla stepped long to reach Meg but Archie jutted his thick arm out blocking her path. Daniel slowly slid forward. Adjusting his position closer to Archie every chance he got. Hoping to go unnoticed.

"You want her back you got to give me something in return."

His cousin sneered. "That is never going to happen again."

"I ain't talking about a roll in the hay. Although those were our best moments."

Daniel crept closer.

"I don't have anything left to give you Archie. I'm on my heels."

He inched along towards Archie.

"Everyone has something to give. The tank is never empty."

Almost there.

Jayla asked, "What do you want from me?"

"Respect," said Archie.

Daniel was close enough. He coiled down a little bending his knees. He checked the room. The mountain held Meg. The fat goon watched his boss. And where did Billy go?

He felt a tap at the small of his back. He looked over his left shoulder to find Billy smiling with his stupid toothpick.

"You want to dance, ugly?" he whispered.

He looked down at where Billy had tapped him. He had a short barrel revolver pointed at his spine. Daniel shook his head no.

"Didn't think so. Now stand still you twitchy shit."

His cousin had registered his and Billy's interaction. Archie hadn't even glanced over. His focus was completely on Jayla. Waiting for her response.

She dropped her shoulders and asked, "How can I show respect?"

"Humility is a start. Another way is to check with me before you make any major life decisions. Like when you decide to bat for the other team."

Daniel got it now. His ego was larger than Archie himself could ever be. Larger than this room could contain. Vaster than the whole county.

"I didn't think you cared what I did anymore."

"We aren't an item anymore. That's true but your actions are still a reflection on me. I can't be seen as a man who's been with a queer. I have my place in the community."

"Again, I ask. How can I show proper respect?"

"First wipe that attitude that you're better than me out of your voice. Understand me?"

Jayla nodded.

"Say yes Archie. I understand."

His cousin took a steadying breath, corrected her slouching posture, and said, "Yes, Archie. I understand."

Archie said, "Good. Now the other thing is the dyke has to go. I mean out of Marion. Preferably out of Kentucky. I don't give a damn where. Just gone."

Meg mumbled something into the rag in her mouth. No doubt a muffled curse. The giant shook her like a rag doll for a second. Her eyes fluttered between conscious and unconscious.

"I need some time to make that happen."

"Time? Sure, since I'll be too busy this weekend with the Slasher Cup, you can have two days. Monday, I see her ass next to your ass. I'll take a different tact. Billy take their pictures."

Billy took out his smartphone and took a photo of Daniel. He said, "Put your glasses back on.

He slid his shades back on and Billy took another picture. He took a quick shot of Jayla then went over to Meg. He said, "Pull her head up." When the big guy yanked her up by the hair, Billy got a snapshot of her bruised-up face. He inspected his phone screen for a sec and then gave his boss the thumbs up.

Archie signaled the giant to let go of Meg. She crumpled to her knees. The giant flipped open a folding knife and roughly cut off her zip cuffs. Meg tried to remove the duct tape gag but her fingers couldn't peel the edge. His cousin looked at Archie and he nodded.

Jayla went over to Meg and helped remove the tape from her mouth. The balled-up rag stuck to the duct tape and pulled out of her mouth. The tape also took some skin off her swollen lips. His cousin motioned for him to come over. They lifted Meg and got under each of her shoulders propping her up.

"We're leaving if that's okay?"

"Asking permission is a sign of respect. You seem to have got the message so yeah it's fine if you take your friends and leave."

They maneuvered Meg to the door. None of the men got out of the way so they had to weave their way around them. Being careful not to brush up against them. Billy waggled his toothpick when Daniel passed by. They finally made it when Archie snapped his fingers.

Archie said, "I'm sending those pics to all my guys. To all of my brother Johnny's guys. And the sheriff. They see the dyke or the tweaker out and about and it's open season on their asses. Come Monday, they better have hit the road for good. Have a nice night"

THIRTEEN

DANIEL DROVE THE TESLA up Aunt Kelly's driveway slowly careful not to kick up gravel. This electric car had teeth. Jayla held Meg in her lap in the small back seat. Meg had wanted to go by and pick up her car before heading back to the house. Jayla said it could wait till the morning and Meg didn't have any fight left in her to argue.

This time it only took one of them to help Meg walk. Daniel being the strongest and the heaviest assisted her inside. He took her directly to the master bedroom at the right rear of the house. Jayla pulled back the comforter and spread it on the four-post bed. He helped Meg's bruised body onto the high mattress. Jayla tucked her in and she rolled her back to them curling up.

No words were spoken during this entire transaction. Daniel thought he should offer some encouraging words though that was not his thing. His cousin held a single finger to her lips silencing his attempt. They both backed out of the room and Jayla shut the door leaving a single lamp on.

Daniel followed Jayla to their Uncle Jonathan's study. She walked right up to the liquor cabinet and pulled out an amber bottle of bourbon. She grabbed two rock glasses and sat behind their uncle's impressive cherry desk. Daniel pulled a dark leather chair and sat on the other side of the desk.

"I'm sorry."

She poured an inch into each glass. She gave her glass another inch. "Archie is the one to be sorry. You didn't do anything."

He took his glass and swished the corn liquor around. "I didn't believe in your cause. This destruction of your ex. But I'm starting to come around."

She sipped from her glass. "And here I thought you were going to give me some spiel about backing out of the job again."

"No. He's got it coming. In spades." He took a long drink of the smoky bourbon.

She toasted her glass to him. "I needed that spirit. But with Meg out of commission. The job's off."

His glass slapped the desktop. "We can do it. Have to hustle a little more but we can pull it off."

"He knows what you look like now. The whole fucking county will be morning. We're burned."

He tugged on his whiskers. "I can shave. Wear some different clothes."

"And if they catch us? He'll hurt you so bad. Twist your skin with pliers. Burn you a little. Then maybe leave you in a hollow to die. I can't risk it now."

"I'm dying slowly anyway." He finished off his glass and slid it toward the bottle.

She poured another inch. "That doctor is helping you. Got you headed in the right direction now."

"When you are so far in the hole, you can't tell if you're going up, down, or in a circle. There's no light to see." He got his glass and took another drink. "I think I was going in a circle until you shone a light."

"Drunk poetry ain't changing my mind. It's over. We're through."

He slapped the desk again. "It ain't over. Not till you get what you want. Not till we all get what we need."

She leaned back in her uncle's leather chair and tented her fingers. "Respect."

He toasted her response. "Not from him. From ourselves."

Jayla leaned back up with her hands together like a prayer. "Let's see how we all feel in the morning. Let Meg have some input. Go get some rest. I'll take care of her."

Daniel didn't argue with her. He finished his glass of bourbon and left the study. He began to go up the stairway to the guestroom but stopped his step on the first rung. The house wasn't lit up like usual but he felt eyes on him outside the windows. He shook off his natural paranoia and drug his tired bones upstairs to bed.

Jayla was behind the wheel of Aunt Kelly's Tesla again. She slowed down as they went past Daddio's Pizza on Poplar Street. He spotted Meg's car on their first drive-by. She turned the car around in St. Benedict's parking lot and they made another pass. He didn't spot anyone hanging around that might be associated with Archie's thugs. His cousin pulled into the Lebanon Junction Water Works and parked.

"Looked clear to me," she said.

He nodded. "I thought so."

"You got the keys ready?"

He jingled the car keys in his hoodie pocket. "All good."

She pointed down the street. "I'm going to pull behind that abandoned house next to the community center by Daddios. You slip around back and get the car. When you leave the lot, honk twice. If you have trouble, just lay on the horn."

"Honk twice for clear. One long sustained honk for trouble. Got it."

She backed the Tesla out. Daniel thought it amusing that they were being sneaky in a one hundred-thousand-dollar car. One so unique in this part of the state that they might as well have been riding a unicorn bareback down Poplar Street. Kentucky was a coal state after all and electric cars were the present and future enemy. The Tesla S was at least a quiet running car. Spooked pedestrians when they caught it in their peripheral vision.

She parked behind the yellow brick two-story house. He got out right away and jumped the rusty fence into the backyard. The grass in the yard came to mid-thigh on him. He made it across the yard and easily leaped over the other fence. He crept past the garbage cans behind the community center. The white paint on the concrete block walls looked like someone had taken a wet cloth and tried to wipe the paint off.

He hid behind a large untrimmed bush at the corner of the building. He could see Meg's car parked at the rear of Daddio's from his position. No puffed-up underlings of Archies to be seen. Daddio's didn't have any windows on the side for anyone to be watching the car. Just a light gray door along the yellow exterior wall of the pizza place. The only other vehicle in the lot was an empty minivan parked out front.

A little after ten in the morning with little traffic on a Saturday morning. Daniel walked briskly from his hiding spot to the car. He had the fob in his pocket. The door would open as soon as he touched the handle. And it worked like a charm. He slid into the driver's seat and shut the door. Jayla told him to place his foot on the brakes and press the ignition button by the steering column. The engine turned over. Barry Manilow sang Mandy through the speaker system.

He smiled as he hoisted on his seat belt. Daniel thought maybe some Bob Seger or ACDC but not this soft rock troubadour. A knock came on his window and he jerked his neck into the canvas seatbelt trying to escape. He threw his arms up as shields waiting for the bat or the bullet to punch through the car window.

"Hay!"

A heavy-set woman in a bright pink sweatshirt waved

at him. Her hair was bright red and curly with the texture of cotton candy. Her smile was just as big as her presence. On the front of the sweatshirt read Daddios.

"Thought you needed a jump but started right up."

He rolled down the window. "Yeah, sorry. We left it here last night. I rode home with friends."

"Had a little too many cervazas, huh? You could have waited till later. We wouldn't have towed it but we were curious."

"Thanks for not calling the police."

"Police. We got three potbellied deputies as law. Barely have a sheriff. Merle would have just hooked a chain on and pulled it to the junkyard." She laughed.

He gave a short wave. "Well, thanks again. I got to get going now."

She cocked a finger pistol at him and winked. "Adios, amigo."

He backed Meg's car out and when he got to the street, he remembered he was supposed to signal his cousin waiting behind the community center. Damned if he could recall how many honks he was supposed to use. He hit the horn three then a fourth time. In his rearview mirror, the lady in pink put her hands on her and toggled her head wondering what the hell he was doing.

He whipped the car in a fast, right-hand turn and drove past the community center. Jayla slipped out right behind him and matched his speed. His cell phone buzzed in his pocket and he flipped open the clamshell to answer it.

"What was that honking? They following you?"

"No, I forgot the signal. There was just a lady who works there."

"Okay. Just got a text from Carl and it ain't good. I'll tell you about it back at Aunt Kelly's" She zoomed silently past him on his left blowing a big cloud of vapor out her window.

He clapped the phone shut and placed it on the center console then he followed his cousin back home to busted plans, broken women, and his own cracked egg.

FOURTEEN

"WHY DID YOU ALL LEAVE ME BEHIND?"

Meg with her puffed-up right cheek and swollen right eye leaned on the mudroom wall. She met them as soon as they came in from the garage. She pushed off the wall and winced but still cut them off from passing.

"I'm still in the game. You can't bench me."

Jayla gently touched Meg's injured cheek. "No one's benching you, honey. We were just letting you rest up."

Meg turned her head away from his cousin's touch. "Cleaning up my mess you mean."

Daniel chose this moment to step past. "I got to take a whiz."

Meg pushed him from behind. There wasn't a lot of strength in it but he turned to face her. "What did I do?"

"Do? You drove my car. I'm the driver. Me! Without me, this job can't be done."

He said, "If you can go, you can drive."

She looked at Jayla. "You hear this shit? Just like a man to think he can boss a woman around."

"We just did this to get the car back and let you rest. You're overthinking things."

Meg squinted her good left eye. "Don't cut me out."

"Honey, even if you can't go on the job tonight, you're still getting your cut. Honest."

"My cut? Meg Jaworski pulls her own weight. You two bitches try to stop me and you'll find out how banged up I am."

Meg limped off from the two cousins. He could have sworn she left a chemtrail of rage in her wake. Meg looked awful. Her color was pale. She favored one leg. She had touched her left ribs like she was holding them together. Her lip split and swollen. But Daniel thought he would have to be in one of his berserker phases to stop her from coming tonight.

"She'll calm down," she said.

"She's going to get herself killed. As damaged as she is, she might get us killed too."

"You going to tell her she can't go?"

"And be pissing blood later? I'll pass."

Jayla said, "Get the gear out of the trunk. I'll go see if I can soothe our savage beast and drag her to the kitchen. We have a change of plans for tonight according to Carl."

He saluted her and went to collect the two duffel bags out of Meg's car trunk. He hoped they had 1980s Arnold Schwarzenegger packed in there. They could use his kind of bombastic help tonight.

"You're sending psycho into the cockfight arena? That's the new plan?" Meg sat in the living room's leather recliner. This is as far as Jayla could drag her out. Besides the kitchen didn't have any soft seats for her bruises.

"Carl said they changed all the locks this morning. Just a random security shit for the big match. Not like they were worried about our lame asses robbing them."

Meg said, "And he can't get a new set of keys?"

"Not by tonight, hon."

"It's over then."

Jayla puffed out some vapor from her pen. "No. I just told you. Carl will take a tour around the arena on his break. Daniel will follow him when he heads back to the cash room. He acts like he's taken Carl hostage with a gun. Just for any cameras or guards, they run into. Then Daniel gets me in the back and we slide into our original plan."

"Archie's guys have our pictures. My picture. I sorta stand out in a crowd." He leaned against the stone fireplace mantle.

His cousin swooped her vape pen. "You can't blend that's for sure but we can make you stand out differently."

He pulled on his chin hair. "I don't know."

"A shave. Slick that hair back. Throw on a sport coat from Uncle Jonathon's closet. You won't be recognizable."

Meg laughed. "You're going to pluck the feathers off this chicken and send him into a cockfight. Brilliant."

"He can do it," said Jayla. "You can do it?"

He wiped his hands off on his Carhartt pants. "Doesn't sound like we got a choice."

His cousin left Meg's side and came over to give him a big hug. Their wounded getaway driver glared at him from behind Jayla's back.

"Now let's go get you spit-polished."

After he cut and shaved his beard off, tried on a few of Uncle Jonathon's clothes his cousin gave her seal of approval, and they all took a break. Jayla and Meg stayed to themselves for the rest of the day. He saw his cousin go into the kitchen and grab some Yoo-hoo and a bag of chips. She took them back to the bedroom. Other than that, it was him by himself in the den channel surfing nervously rubbing his smooth ugly jaw. He kept checking the weather for tonight. Cloudy with temperatures falling into the low fifties.

He got antsy so he went down to the basement where Jayla said his uncle he had never met had a fitness room. A flip of the switch and the room illuminated. He believed his aunt used the room as well but it had a masculine feel to it. Posters of what else but Kentucky Wildcat athletes. A black poster with a blocky white type that read "Pain

Is Just Weakness Leaving the Body". He didn't like all the attention from the one wall of floor-to-ceiling mirrors.

But damned if there wasn't a heavy bag in the corner. It was black vinyl and didn't have duct tape holding it together like his but Daniel was sure glad to see it hanging there. He took off his hoodie and hung it off the Stairmaster. Some fancy blue bag gloves were resting on a dumbbell rack. He slid them on and pounded his palms with them to make sure of the fit. He was ready to swing.

He flicked some quick left jabs out testing his distance and the bag's suppleness. The bag was rigid. Seldom used as he suspected. He threw a hard-right cross then a harder hook lower into the body of the bag. Left, right, left. Faster combos building rhythm. He saw the person he was hitting. He saw them slip his jabs.

He brought his hands back to his cheeks protecting himself after every punch. Training his muscle memory so he did the right thing even when he was tired. And a puncher's arms get weary. Someone told him boxing was like jogging on your arms. Drained your tank quickly. Vary your punches, use strategy then unleash in a flurry of combos. That's how he trained.

But that's not reality. He watched his gas station fight on video. He was unorthodox in his strikes. He kicked. He used elbows and head butts. He even bit that guy. He recalled past skirmishes where he grabbed the nearest object at hand and used it as a force multiplier to beat someone into submission. He was an undisciplined animal.

Dr. Rhiney said we have untapped potential in us.

Latent abilities waiting to spring out. She might have meant useful skills like business savvy or artistic talents. He couldn't help thinking this whirling dervish of violence was his. Maybe with some focused training, he could control his brutish ways. Use them in a directed manner on command. That could be a useful skill but he couldn't tell his therapist she was helping him train the berserker inside.

He would need control tonight when they robbed Archie's club. He was proud of how he had kept it together last night in the office. It felt tighter than a pressure cooker in there. And he hadn't exploded. Dr. Rhiney did say exposing himself to more scenarios that could cause him to lash out might also present a chance to work on his resolve. Through effort and certain techniques like breathing, his mind became in charge of his actions. The daily pills didn't hurt either.

His punches slowed down and he found himself wringing wet with sweat. He had been looking for something to take the edge off and now he was spent. His rich uncle even had a small refrigerator with a glass door in his home gym. It was stocked with orange Gatorade, Evian bottled water, and Michelob Ultra beer. He took an orange sports drink out and drank sloppily. He used his shirt collar to wipe his lips.

He took in the room while he walked to the door. Could he ever have a life like this with a private gym and an electric car? Did he even want to? He had other questions he needed to ponder as well. Daniel flicked off the lights and went upstairs to refresh with a well-earned nap.

FIFTEEN

THEY WERE IN THE KITCHEN at 9 pm. He and his cousin had cleaned up the house. Next to the two olive army duffel bags on the table was a sealed envelope containing a letter for their aunt. After tonight they wouldn't be coming back to Aunt Kelly's place. They would be on the run.

Jayla wore black jeans and a matching sweatshirt. She also had an oversized black nylon jacket that you could buy cheaply at Walmart. He had a spacious nylon jacket too. She handed him a ski mask to try on. Taking his big framed glasses off, he put the mask on. It wasn't scratchy and his vision wasn't blocked but he wouldn't be able to wear his sunglasses with the mask.

"You should have asked me to bring my luchador masks."

"Shiny sequins don't exactly blend into the darkness."

"Point taken but they would be freaked out if they saw us in them."

"We don't want people freaked out. If things go as planned, we'll only see Carl then Maria, and Ellis counting cash in the back room. Need everyone to stay chill."

"Why doesn't Archie have like fifty men guarding the money?"

"He has his law dogs and regular guys doing the close-in and security perimeter. Plus, all the big betters work for the El Mencho cartel or the Kentucky Fried Mafia. Anyone would be crazy to steal from dangerous criminals like them."

He slid his mask up over his forehead. "That's us. Crazy Incorporated."

She tried on her mask. "How do I look?"

He tucked her long hair under the mask. "Like a gas station stick-up man. What about me?"

He wore a dark denim shirt under a beige sport coat and black jeans. His uncle had some amber-framed designer sunglasses that didn't cover as much of his bug eyes as his big black frames did but they did give him some mental relief. With his hair slicked back, his Mom wouldn't recognize him.

She said, "I think we got a chance."

Meg limped into the kitchen twisting back and forth at the waist. "I think you got it taped too tight. Can you take a look?"

She immediately pulled her red t-shirt over her head leaving the bunched-up shirt around her neck. She wore a tight Nike sports bra. Around her torso was an elastic ace bandage wrap. She undid the clips and started to unwind them. Jayla moved to help her.

"Hold on idiot. It's supposed to be tight."

Meg whined, "Not this tight. I can't breathe."

"If you're talking, you're breathing." His cousin corralled the unwound wrapping and placed it on the table. Meg's rib area was taped up with white medical tape and it appeared to be some gray tape too.

Daniel said, "You used duct tape?"

"Ran out of the medical tape." She inspected Meg's makeshift bandages running her hand around the seams.

"Rotate bitch."

That got a smile out of Meg as she pirouetted. Jayla checked the rest of her tape job.

"Looks fine. You need it tight to support your ribs."

"Leave the ace wrap off then." Meg pulled her t-shirt back on.

"Don't complain later when the tape loosens and sticks to your shirt." She rolled up the elastic bandage into a tight roll. She tossed it into an open duffel bag.

Meg said, "We should boost another car. Billy might have seen what I was driving at that pizza place."

"You said he caught you right outside the door. He couldn't know what car you were driving, right?" His cousin opened the refrigerator and got out three bottles of water.

"Unless he followed me there. We need a different car." She waved off Jayla's offer of water.

"You are not well enough to go stealing cars. And

there's no time to now." Jayla put the bottles of water in the duffel bag without offering Daniel one and zipped it up. He wasn't thirsty anyway.

"There is another option." Meg glanced at the garage.

His cousin scrunched up her face. "No. I'm not taking any of Aunt Kelly's cars."

"We can leave it somewhere for her to pick up later."

Jayla shook her head. "Not happening."

Meg said, "I won't put a scratch on any of her fancy cars."

Daniel laughed. "Sorry."

Meg tried to limp around the kitchen island to confront him but Jayla stepped in her way.

"We stick to our plan and take your car. I already owe Aunt Kelly too much." She patted Meg on her chest and kissed her on her frowning lips.

Daniel picked up both duffel bags off the counter. One had water and clothing. The other one was heavy with guns and more clothes.

He said, "Let's go rob us some chicken-fighting idiots."

Daniel led the way out of the house. He put the bags in the trunk while Jayla got in the driver's seat and Meg got in the passenger's side. He slammed the trunk shut and got in the rear seat of the car which might betray them later. His cousin turned the car around and drove down the elevated driveway. He looked back and watched the best place he ever slept in getting smaller and smaller.

They drove back to Lebanon by way of the Bluegrass Parkway and then to US 150. They went through

Springfield and approached from the north on US 55. Took almost an hour to get back to the seat of Marion County. A sleepy downtown. It would be all lit up next weekend during the Ham Festival. The place would be jumping with locals and out-of-towners. They passed as quietly through as they could. Not looking to be seen or unseen.

Daniel had seen enough of Marion County and this part of Kentucky. He was ready to go back to Louisville right this second if his cousin decided to back out. She hadn't blinked so far. Her wheelman lover rode in the passenger seat. Her ugly powder keg of a cousin dumbfounded in the back. And Jayla still drove to their potential last hurrah. She was just a taller version of the impetus ten-year-old he ran with through flint-bottomed creeks.

He brought his attention back to the drive. They rounded off Josh Creek Rd. So dark if they turned the headlights out reality would shift only to the dashboard lights. This way didn't seem like last night's drive to the Bluegrass Sports Club. Last night was get there quick. Tonight was get there unnoticed. They hadn't passed any other car so far since they left Lebanon.

The road turned into a steep climb. When they reached the pinnacle, Jayla turned their headlights off and took a left onto a dirt road that didn't have a mailbox. The running lights were still illuminated just enough for his cousin to guide the car. Tall tree branches made a leafy tunnel they drove under. After a good mile or two, she parked the car on the side of the dirt road in the grass facing the way they came in.

"You'll walk in from here. Can't risk them seeing the car or us together." Jayla checked her smartphone face. "Find Carl in the arena by the red corner table then come let me in."

"What if Archie, Billy, or any other of them recognize me?"

"Improvise and get the fuck out. I need this money but I don't need a dead cousin."

He could see Meg sweating even in the darkened car. His cousin put her hand on the seat between them. "Alright everyone hands in the middle."

He placed his hand on top of hers. Meg reluctantly stacked her hand on top of his.

Jayla said, "On the count of three, stay frosty. One, two, three."

They all called out 'stay frosty' then Meg pulled her hand back sharply. His cousin gave him a 'what are you going to do' look. "Good luck."

He got out of the car and walked up the dirt road towards the club. He heard them turn the car around and leave but he didn't look back. The dark road soon was lit up by the Bluegrass Sports Club parking lot. It was brighter than the last night. The place looked like a pick-up truck sales lot. There must be four hundred trucks parked tonight. At the entrance, a bright blue Dodge Ram idled vapor lightly streaming out his tailpipe. A man in a heavy plaid shirt and an orange ballcap stepped out of the cab.

"Howdy fella."

Daniel said, "Evening."

"That'll be ten dollars." He held his hand out.

Daniel produced the VIP pass that Jayla had given him earlier. It would allow him entry without buying a ticket and access to most parts of the club that the general admission folk wouldn't receive.

"Yeah, that's for inside. Still, ten dollars to park." The man's hand was still out.

Daniel cocked his head. "I got dropped off. Ain't parking anything."

"Rules are rules. You're using the lot so I gotta have the tenner."

Daniel dug out his wallet and handed the man two five-dollar bills.

"Hope you got the big bills in your front pocket. They don't take credit cards inside."

Daniel patted his breast coat pocket. "Keep it close to my heart."

The man tipped his hat. "Enjoy the Kentucky Gamefowl Derby, sir."

Daniel left the literal man at his post. He crossed the parking lot and made it to the entrance. In the VIP parking slots were some luxury model SUVS of different makes and models. License plates from Illinois, Michigan, Tennessee, Maryland, and others. Jayla said they sell as many roosters as they fight at the match. They bet in the stands between each other. The big money went through Archie's tellers. Daniel felt better that they were ripping off the haves and not the have-nots in the stands.

There were some men gathered in the cold outside smoking and drinking. Most were small groups of good old boys. Three Mexican men of indeterminate age stood apart from the others. They wore stylish clothes. One said something to another one in Spanish as they watched him pass. They broke out in laughter when he opened the club door.

A cacophony of people cheering and fighting cocks crowing assaulted his ears when he stepped inside. It was warm and bright. The air was thick with smoke from cigarettes and cigars. Foul but he found it oddly comforting compared to Jayla's mint vaping. A second whiff brought in the scent of a chicken coop and stale sweat. A Kentucky State Trooper in full regalia guarded the main entrance to the arena.

Daniel crossed the lobby to the ticket booth his cousin pointed out last night. He presented his VIP pass to an old lady manning the post. A filterless cigarette dangled from her mouth. "Hold it up to the glass."

He placed the pass flat on the glass between them. She took an iPad and scanned a bar code on his pass. Pretty sophisticated for a cockfight he thought. The old lady looked satisfied and said, "Just show the pass to Trooper Rick. He'll let you in. Have a good one."

Trooper Rick let him pass into the arena proper. The place was darkly lit except for the center cockfighting ring. A large circle of lights haloed above it casting gleaming light down on the two handlers in the ring backing up their prized roosters. He ambled closer to the center ring to get a better look. He passed another guard. This time a Marion County Deputy. Daniel just showed him his pass and he let him walk past the velvet ropes with the other VIPs.

The ring was round and elevated. He stood to the side and watched a couple of long-legged roosters size each other up. They both flared their black neck feathers into an aggressive mane. Metal gaffs attached to their heels glinted in the strong overhead lighting. The gamefowl both launched at the same time extending their spurs at the other. Fast, furious, and blood was let on both sides. The large one on the left look like he got the worst of it.

His handler picked up the bird and put its whole head in his mouth. The man looked to be sucking on the rooster. He pulled the bird's head out of his mouth and he spat blood on the dirt floor. He set the cock back down on the ground facing his opponent and blew on his tail feathers. That rooster shot across that ring for his pound of revenge. Daniel looked away but heard the clink of the metal spurs. Loud cheers went up.

He was searching for the red table that Carl was supposed to be at when he noticed Archie sitting ringside next to a large bearded man in bib overalls and a straw cowboy hat. Daniel felt a little overdressed until he saw some of the other VIP attendees were dressed up. In the general admission seating, the clothing was denim jeans, boots, and Kentucky Wildcat shirts. He saw Billy in the top row of the bleachers. He received a lot of public affection from some country honey.

Someone bumped him and said, "Pardon me." Daniel went to respond and saw that it was Carl. Their inside man just nodded his head and walked over to the far corner from the concession stand to a red table. He lit up a cigarette and drank from a paper cup. No one watched him approach Carl's table. All eyes were on the center pit.

Daniel pointed to the other chair at the table. Carl nodded for him to sit. He didn't look nervous at all. "Looking spiffy kid. Still hard on the eyes but spiffy. Wasn't sure if you had the stones to show up."

"How did you know this table would be empty?"

"It's red. These Wildcat fans wouldn't be caught dead in red. They leave it for me. The colored fellow. Because I have to be a Louisville Cardinal fan like the rest of the darkies."

"If it sucks so bad here why don't you just leave?"

"I expect you said the same dumb shit to your cousin too."

He slid his hand across his jutting chin. "I did."

Carl nodded. "Ain't options for every one kid. You should know better than others."

His neck got a little flushed. Must have shown more than he thought because Carl held up his hands.

"Not your fault you were born ugly. Or I was born black in Crackerville. We just have to deal with the cards we've been dealt now. This is how I play my hand."

Daniel calmed a little. "Let's play then."

"Heard you met Archie last night." Carl pointed with his cigarette. "You see him over there by the pit?"

"I caught a glimpse of him."

"That Spanish fell to his left is Abraham Morales. That cockfighting fan is a distant cousin to El Mencho."

"El Mencho?"

"Leader of a cartel out of west Mexico. The guys who

like to give acid baths and chop heads off when they ain't moving meth and fentanyl around the U.S of A."

Daniel hissed, "Easy."

"And the bearded guy to his right. That's Johnny Mudd himself. Head of the legendary Kentucky Fried Mafia." He took a pull on his cigarette and exhaled the smoke out his nose. "Still want to play?"

"I'm duly warned and I've pissed my pants. But as you said earlier, ain't options for everyone."

The older black man stubbed out his cigarette in an ashtray and stood up. "Stand close to me as we walk. That way I can say you had a gun on me the whole time. You do have a gun?"

Daniel patted his right coat pocket feeling the heaviness of the automatic pistol. "After you."

Carl walked in front with Daniel just a touch away on his left hip. They went through the double doors into the lobby. He patted Trooper Rick on the shoulder as they passed by. At the closed doors that led to the hallway and the back rooms, Carl waved to the old lady smoking in the ticket booth. She read from a romance novel and barely looked up but she slipped her hand under the counter. A buzzer went off and a loud click as the doors unlocked.

Inside the hallway, Daniel remembered to the left was Archie's office. Carl led him further down the hallway. Almost going the full distance. There were two doors spaced out ten feet apart on the left. And one on the right. The right door was the cash room. Home of the big bets. At the end of the hall was a door. Bright new chrome chains wrapped around it.

"Don't look but there are cameras on us. Only recording and no audio. I'm going to need you to rough me up a little. Push me towards the back door."

It went against his nature but Daniel shoved the old man hard. Carl stumbled and look back at him with fear in his eyes. The old man was cagey.

"Time to show me the gun kid," he said through his fearful grimace.

Daniel pulled his gun out and pointed it at the old man. He felt a little wooden. "Let her in or I'll blast you."

Carl raised his hands selling his compliance. He turned his back on Daniel and was going towards the door he laughed. "Hope your acting improves inside the room. Them folks already work for a scary dude."

Daniel reached out and pulled Carl back by the shoulder of his jacket. He pushed him into the wall and screwed the barrel of his pistol into his exposed neck. "This better."

Carl's eyes were wide. "Academy award-winning."

Daniel flung him at the door. Carl fumbled with a set of keys and undid the padlocks on the chains and then the door lock itself. The door slowly opened and his cousin wearing a ski mask in all black handed him a duffle bag. She trained her gun on Carl as Daniel put his ski mask over his head.

"Howdy Carl."

"Miss Durand."

Daniel got his eyeholes lined up and said, "Let's roll."

Jayla grabbed the old man roughly and shoved him in the direction of the cash room door. Carl went reluctantly.

This was all an act. A bad seventies heist movie. Daniel played his part nervously watching the end of the open hallway towards Archie's office. Carl knocked out a rhythmic sequence onto the door to the cash room. A voice said, "Check one?"

Carl said, "Big Crow Lake."

The voice asked, "Check two?"

He responded, "Eight, twenty-one, two-thousand and nineteen."

The voice said, "Opening the door."

When the door started to open, Daniel put all his weight into a big push kick with the flat of his boot. The metal door thwacked into the person behind it. A satisfying solid sound. He entered the room with his drawn gun pointed at the floor. Jayla swept in after him. A stout young man holding his busted nose on the floor. His pistol handle jutted out from a sidearm holster rig under his left arm.

"Don't fucking move!" Daniel took the gun from his holster and stuck it in his waistband.

"Hands on your head and face the wall."

The guy took his hands from his bleeding nose and laced the fingers onto his head. He started to get up but Daniel kicked him back down.

"Un uh. Scoot around on your ass." Daniel did a twist motion with his pistol.

The bleeding man with murder in his eyes scooted around to face the wall. Daniel asked, "Everything cool back there?"

His cousin said, "As a cucumber."

Daniel glanced back and saw her holding three people in place by pointing her gun in their direction. One person was a saucer-eyed Carl. Damn, he was a world-class actor. Daniel took some zip ties they bought at the hardware store and went up to the fallen guard. He nudged the barrel into the back of his head.

"Heroes get their heads blown off. Understand?" His voice cracked when he spoke.

The guard said, "Yeah."

"Good. Lower your hands behind your back slowly."

The man complied and Daniel slipped the do-it-yourself zip cuffs over the man's wrists and pulled tight. The guy sat up straight from the pain. Daniel pressed down on his shoulder.

"Easy hoss." Daniel took a roll of duct tape and carefully wrapped it around his mouth leaving his nostrils open.

After gagging the guard, he took out a black pillowcase and placed it over the bleeder's head. That move elicited a rumbling from the man. Daniel kneed him roughly between the shoulder blades. The man calmed down. Daniel turned to help his cousin deal with her group tucking his gun in his pocket. His hands trembled once he wasn't holding them.

She said, "Everyone get over there and face the wall like he's doing."

They were all frozen. Carl tipped his head a little. Daniel took that as his cue and punched Carl hard in the stomach. He then grabbed him roughly by his collar and belt tossing Carl across the room onto the floor by the guard. Daniel turned his head to the two women. They stumbled across the room to take their place on the wall.

His cousin said, "Hands behind your back."

Daniel zip-cuffed them starting on the left. The women breathed rapidly. Carl uttered a curse word when he got cuffed. Daniel bumped his head into the wall.

"Knock it off." Daniel gagged all of them with duct tape and then put black pillowcases over every one of their heads.

"Get down on the floor and face the fucking wall. Knees or ass. Now!" His cousin's voice was strained.

The three office workers finally got to the ground and settled. Daniel finally got a look at what they were there for. Two long card tables with stacks of wrapped cash. There were loose stacks of unwrapped cash. A laptop next to a ledger with handwritten notes. A couple of light gray machines that looked similar to printers and some dollar bills in a rack. He had seen one of these in a movie once. Currency counters.

"Come on get the bags open." She nudged him out of his revelry.

He unfolded one duffel on the table to his left. She immediately started shoving cash into the bag. He shook his bag open and got the loading it with money from the other table. He was sweating under his mask something fierce. And he started to feel like he was leaving his body. Just for a minute, his perspective was looking down on him and his cousin shoveling reams of chicken-fighting cash into worn duffel bags.

A knock at the door snapped him back into his body.

Jayla looked at Daniel. He could see the shock in her eyes. He grabbed her by the shoulder and pulled her over to the hostages.

He spoke in hushed tones to the group on the floor. "Stay quiet and no one gets hurt."

His cousin acted squirrelly. Her nerves taking over. He whispered to her. "Watch them. I'll take care of this."

"I'm sorry."

"Don't be sorry. Be ready," he growled. He could feel the heat coming from his shoulders. His badness was rising.

Another loud knock on the door. She hung the duffel bag around her neck and shoulder. She took out her pistol and held it close to her leg pointing at the floor. He nodded and held up his hand counting to three on his fingers. When he reached three, he spoke.

"Check one?"

"It's me. Tony."

"Okay, Tony. Check one?"

"Dammit, Bruce open the fuck up. It's me." The man outside banged on the door.

"Archie's rules, man. Check one?"

"Uh, Big Crow Lake?"

Daniel looked back at Jayla. She moved offline from him a little taking a knee and using it to help steady her aim as she pointed her pistol at where the door would open.

Daniel asked, "Check two?"

"Let's see. Eight and something. It's a bunch of numbers. Just open the door!"

"Go get the right numbers and I'll open it."

The voice on the other side of the door boomed, "I'm going asshole!"

Daniel waited for a good count of thirty Mississippis. Opening the door slowly, he peeked his head out. The long hallway was empty. He waved come on to his cousin and she popped up from her kneeling. He went out first covering the hallway towards the event area. Jayla moved swiftly to the door they came in. He kept his eyes on the dangerous end of the hallway but backpedaled to join her.

He heard the seal on the door squeak when she opened it. She patted him on the shoulder and he almost fired his gun.

She said, "Clear. Let's go."

They popped out the door and loaded up the four-wheel ATV's front and rear racks. Bungee cords held the duffel bags fast to the rack frames. His cousin took out the vehicle's key from her pocket, stuck it in the ignition, and saddled up in the driver's position. He laced his leg over the seat and tucked in behind her. The ATV rumbled to a start on the first push of the button. Jayla pulled the clutch handle into neutral with her left hand and fed it some gas with a twist of her right wrist.

Daniel was afraid that the revving would attract a guard or someone but no one appeared. His cousin gave the ATV a little more gas and they took off in a rush. Jayla shifted gears with her left foot as she picked up speed to climb the hilly path back to Meg and their car. It was almost over. He leaned back and let the rushing air cool him under his hot mask. Looking up he watched the clouds through the canopy of tree branches.

The ATV bounced and he had to grab hold of his cousin's jacket to keep it from being thrown off. She howled, "Hold on!"

They came to the end of the path. It didn't lead out of the woods. Who builds a path that stopped forty feet from the tree line? Another unanswered question he would have to reconcile with. He hopped off the ATV and hefted his duffel bag onto his shoulder. Jayla turned the engine off and got her bag off the vehicle rack. They hightailed it through the last forty feet of the brush to their getaway car.

They stopped at the edge of the woods to see if anyone was waiting in the car. Meg pulled her ski mask off. He rolled it up so he could see but still wore his mask. No lights. No one was around. He couldn't see Meg's head sticking up. Where was she?

"Looks safe. Let's go," said his cousin.

"Are you sure? I can't see Meg."

"Bad angle but I don't see anyone else around." She stood up and walked over to the car.

Daniel followed her. He didn't get his special feeling that he was being watched. Something was off though. His cousin peaked into the car and dropped her bag to quickly open the driver's door. He rushed over to the open door. The moonlight made deep shadows in the car since the dome light was disabled. Meg had slipped to the floorboard in a heap.

"She's not responding. Help me pull her up."

He went around to the passenger's door, opened it, and helped hoist Meg onto the seat. She was slick with sweat on her bare skin and her breathing was shallow. Jayla patted her cheek a little.

"Meg? Honey? Wake up."

Hard to see in the dark but her eyes seemed to move under her lids. Daniel felt her forehead. "She's burning up. We need to get her to the hospital."

"She's tough. She'll be okay." His cousin's voice cracked.

"They might have busted something inside her. She could be septic."

Jayla hooked Meg into the seatbelt shoulder harness keeping her upright and secure. "Take her to the Marion County ER? Just show up in ski masks and pay cash. Is that your idea?"

"We don't know how bad this is?"

"That's right we don't." Jayla backed out her door.

He shut the passenger door as quietly as he could. His cousin had her bag and headed to the rear of the car. He met her with his bag in the open trunk. She heaved her bag into the trunk. She peeled off her jacket, balled it up, and tossed it in the trunk too. He placed his bag next to her and roughly folded his jacket then dropped it in the trunk.

Jayla shut the trunk door but leaned on it with her eyes squeezed shut. "Do you think she could die?"

"What are our options? Closest hospital is here. Or ride to Louisville? Stop at an ER there."

"She's tough."

Daniel stroked his whiskered chin. It was damp from wearing the mask. "Like a two-dollar steak."

"Meg wouldn't want to ruin the job."

"We aren't Meg," he said.

"She'll have to make it to Louisville. She stays here and Archie or the KFM will get a hold of her." She hot-stepped it around the car to the driver's seat.

Daniel read the implication. Some things were worse than death. He got into the back seat and slid over behind Meg. He leaned up, and felt her forehead and cheek. Still hot with sweat. He used a hand towel from the back seat to dry her brow. Jayla started the car and drove back down the dark dirt road they came in on.

She still had the lights off when she turned right onto the paved asphalt of Josh Creek Road. She drove slowly down the incline allowing the car to pick up speed. At the bottom of the incline, they both held their breath as they passed the entrance to the Bluegrass Sports Club. No one waited for them. As the car rolled by, no one gave chase. Everything was quiet. Jayla still didn't turn the headlights on till five minutes later.

The adrenaline had been leaving his body since they reached the car. He yawned this time from exhaustion and not nerves. His body had expended all its reserve energy and wanted to rest. They still had over an hour to drive before they made it to the outskirts of Louisville. He put his hand on his cousin's shoulder and gave a gentle squeeze.

"You okay to drive?"

She said, "I'll make it."

He patted her shoulder then. "If you need a break, let me know."

"I will. Thanks."

She turned on the radio and tuned it to an alternative rock channel. She kept the volume low. Just white noise. That didn't help him stay awake. He fell back against the seat leaning his head to the right against the window. The oh-so-cool window was refreshing. Still, his eyelids began to shutter.

Jayla said, "We pulled it off, didn't we?"

He lolled back to an upright position. "The Kentucky Rangers ride again."

She looked over at Meg. "It was almost perfect."

"She'll pull through. Louisville has better hospitals than Marion County."

His cousin fed the car some gas and pushed their top speed up. He said, "Careful, no need for all of us to be checked into the ER."

"Am I too dangerous?"

He fished his sunglasses out of his pocket and put them on. "Always."

She checked him out in the rearview mirror and laughed. "Buckle up then. We got to save my gal."

SIXTEEN

THE LIGHTS WERE SHARP AND BRIGHT lancing off the chrome-edged furniture in the Suburban Hospital ER waiting room. The beams almost pierced his super-dark sunglasses. Daniel knew you could never tell what time of day it was in the hospital. They were lit up as much as a casino in Las Vegas. The antiseptic medicinal odors mixed with the body funk of patients too. Two of his biggest senses were assaulted. He would rather be sweeping the baboon habitat at the zoo for scat than this. He hated doctors.

That wasn't true because he had affection for Dr. Rhiney. He just hated medical doctors. His Mom took him to see a cadre of different doctors when he was younger. Trying to see if they could fix his eyes and face. Lots of tests for nothing. He was stuck with his gargoyle visage. Daniel never knew if his Mom was doing this to help him have a better life or so she didn't have to stare at her little mistake.

He found that written in a spiral notebook she used as a diary when he was twelve. She had called him her 'little mistake'. Daniel was what happened when she sinned with that stranger who was his father. He had finally heard the tale when he was older and she was deep into her alcoholic whims. He was sixteen and begged to know who his father was. She hadn't mentioned him in all the years.

She hadn't because she didn't know who he was. Drunk and fed up with his needling, she told him she slept with an older man she met at a bowling alley. There was no courtship. No dating. It was one night of sin. And Daniel was the ugly reminder of her weakness to everyone. He wanted to leave that night but he stuck it out for two more years till he finished high school. He left the day after graduation and never came home.

Every few months he would check in with his Mom. And every time it was a mistake. Dr. Rhiney wanted him to bring her to a session but he didn't want his space inhabited by that hateful woman. Daniel would step foot on his mother's turf but she wasn't allowed in any of his private places. Home, work, and especially not his therapist's office.

Jayla came through the double doors leading back into the ER rooms. Her eyes were red from crying. Her shoulders slumped. She walked over in her zombie state and sat next to him on the uncomfortable hospital furniture. He wrapped an arm around her shoulders.

"She's going to be okay." She said in a release of breath.

"That's great. Right?"

His cousin started to tear up again. "They have to do surgery. They think her liver has ruptured. Some blood leaking into her abdominal cavity."

He pulled her closer. "It'll work out. Doctors do this all the time."

"It's my fault. Archie is my fault. And everyone else gets hurt but him."

He wiped her eyes with his hoodie sleeve. "We hurt him tonight. And his KFM buddies will take a hunk of his hide for restitution."

"He's got it coming. And that was last night."

He blinked heavily. "Jesus. Is it daytime?"

Jayla showed him the clock face on her cell phone. It read 7:12 am.

He said, "We've been here five hours?"

"Every last minute of it." She got lost in her jean jacket willing it larger. Women have a great ability to do that.

"Is she getting out soon?"

She shook her head. "No, they're still prepping for surgery."

"What happens after that?"

She took a deep breath. "If everything goes alright, she will be in recovery for a couple of days at least."

"Then you all head to Canada?"

She slouched down into her seat. "Vancouver. But yeah as soon as the doc says she can leave we're out of here."

He nudged her knee with his. "You all could stay in Louisville while she recovers. Might be too hard a trip on old Meg's jacked-up liver."

She nudged him back. "Good idea but Meg will want to scat. And this may be two counties over but it's still Kentucky. Archie or his bosses have a reach that extends here too."

He kind of sat up. "Maybe I should come to Canada."

She frowned. "You'll be okay. They don't know you like they know me. Hell, you were two different versions of yourself. Grow your beard back. Just don't be buying caddy's or nothing."

He stroked his clean jawline. "We ain't even counted the money yet."

"Think it's safe in the car? Be ironic if we got our car boosted after all our troubles."

He said, "I don't know about ironic but it would be our family karma."

It took some effort and a helping hand from Daniel but she got up from her seat. She stretched her back and said, "I'm going to check with the staff again. Then I'll take you home. Divvy up the money."

"Ain't no rush Jayla. I can hang out here with you."

"We'd just be waiting around smelling stinky. And I would like to see how much we got to. Hospital bills are expensive. Be right back."

She went back into the ER proper through the double doors. A security guard leaned on the check-in desk talking to the pretty ER admission clerk. Daniel stood up and stretched his legs. He made his way over to the hallway that leads to the parking lot. He walked to the sliding glass doors seeking the warmth of the natural morning light.

Daniel had the duffel bags on his basement floor. He had banded and loose bills on his coffee table. He counted the singles into denominations. Ones, fives, tens, twenties, fifties, and hundreds. There were even some two-dollar bills. He planned on keeping those. Shingo Takagi wrestled Juice Robinson on his tv screen. The sound was muted.

He could hear the water running in his shower. His cousin cleaning off last night's grime. He would have to wait twenty minutes for the water to heat back up again but he was so wrung out a cold shower might be refreshing. His toes were even sore from all the tension. Jayla would keep her shower brief. He knew she wanted to get back to the hospital as soon as she could.

He wrote some more numbers down on the yellow legal pad he had on his couch. The pencil picked up the tremor that began in his hindbrain and traveled through his nervous system down his arm into his fingers. This was a lot of money. Three hundred and fifty-six thousand so far. And he still had most of the second duffel bag to count.

People were killed for a lot less than this. He had seen one man when he was in holding choke out another inmate to steal his phone card. Daniel couldn't deny he had latent violent tendencies but he never was motivated by money. His stomach felt queasy from nerves. What the hell would he do with his cut?

Juice had applied his Pulp Friction finishing move on Shingo. An inverted double under hook facebuster. This pile of stolen money had the same effect on Daniel at this moment. Defeated at the enormity of it all. What was he thinking would happen? That Jayla and he would have happily ever after lives now. Getting the money seemed the easy part. Living with it bore an incredible amount of weight he hadn't anticipated.

"How much?" His cousin toweled her hair dry in the bathroom doorway.

Startled from his thoughts, he stuttered. "Too fucking much."

"Seriously, what's the count so far?" She was back in her leggings and wore a new black t-shirt with an American flag on it.

"Three hundred and fifty. But I still have some more to go."

"That's all?"

He tapped his pencil on the legal pad. "All? Any amount over fifty thousand is life-changing for either one of us."

She dried behind her ears and hung the towel on the doorknob. "It costs a lot to make a new life. Especially in another country."

"Yeah, I don't get that whole Canada thing. Why not

stay here in Louisville? Or just move out west to some small town in Colorado?"

She came over to the couch and sat next to him. "Meg knows some people in Canada. We're going to start a business up there."

Daniel side-eyed his cousin. "Entrepreneurship huh? What kind? Thieves R Us?"

"A legit enterprise. We are going to be partners in a ball-bearing company."

His mouth opened a little. "A ball bearing company?"

She laughed. "A family friend of Meg's owns a small ball-bearing manufacturing facility up north. They are willing to let us buy in and learn the business. Eventually for us to take over."

He slid his pencil into an ice pick hold. "That's the most sensible thing I've ever heard you say. Now you shapeshifting son of a bitch, before I stab you, what have you done with my cousin?"

She bent over and grabbed her boots. She slipped her right foot in and tugged. "What are you going to do with your money?"

He jabbed the eraser end of his pencil into his thigh. "I'm not sure I want any of it."

She had her left boot almost on but stopped to look at him. "You're taking your cut."

He dropped the pencil on the coffee table. "I just. It's a lot of money."

"You earned your share." She finished putting on her boot. Done with him. She got out her vape pen and sucked in some mint-flavored nicotine. She released a big plume making her head almost disappear.

He waved his hand between them. "Something doesn't feel right."

She took the remote and turned the TV off. "It doesn't feel right because you've never had money before. This is how lottery winners feel."

He nodded. "Do lottery winners have the KFM after them? Or El Mencho?"

"No, but they have friends, family, charitable organizations, and other hucksters after their loot. Don't kid yourself. No matter how you earn it people will still try to take your money."

"I don't know. I just felt different before the money. Like I was helping you out. I never even considered how the money would affect me."

She took his hand in hers. "You have helped me. So much. I understand you're having trouble wrapping your head around your sudden wealth but you're taking your share. I'll put it in a bag and bury it in your yard when you aren't looking."

He pulled his hand free. "Maybe I'll donate it."

"That's up to you." She took another pull on her vape pen.

He got up off the couch. "You finish counting up. My totals are on the legal pad. I'm going to take my shower now."

"You sure? Going to be cold as hell."

He took the wet towel off the doorknob so he could

shut the door. He said, "That's a funny saying. Maybe it's true."

There was a flash of hot water before it went cold. The bracing chill woke him up. Raised goose pimples on his flesh. But as soon as he toweled his body dry, the weariness set back in. He combed his long hair back straight. His eyes looked larger and buggier in the light of his mirror. He slid the vanity mirror to the left and shook out two pills from an orange plastic bottle.

He popped them in his mouth, ran some water from the faucet, and bent over to take a swig. He swallowed down the mood stabilizers. The thought of all that money on his coffee table came rushing back in. The pills needed to step up their game if he was to get any sleep later. He put on clean khaki Carhartt pants and a worn white t-shirt.

He thought about his idea of donating the money. He thought about buying a car first. Maybe not a flashy one. Just some plain old reliable car to get him from point A to point B. Be nice to go to the grocery and not have to worry about his Chunky Monkey ice cream melting on the bus ride home. Okay, just a car then he would donate the rest.

He opened the door and said, "Hey, I've decided I'll buy a car, after all, my bitching."

His words fell on an empty room. Jayla was gone. The two duffel bags were gone. All that was left was a stack of money on his coffee table. He could smell the mint from her vape pen too. He walked over and plopped down on his couch.

Next to the bills was his legal pad. Pretty cursive words were written on it. He picked up the pad and read it.

Daniel,
The total count was $515,023. I left you $170,000. Plus all your stupid 2 dollar bills. Thanks for helping me when I needed it. You're the best cousin ever. The only real friend I have outside of Meg. I know I'm not the easiest person to help. Wasn't like I asked you for a ride to work. We don't see each other for ten years then I ask you to rob a cock-fighting ring. LOL. They can't say I'm boring. Anyway, thanks again. I have really missed you all these years and this short time together will make me miss you even more but I have to leave. Don't come to the hospital. Don't call me. Right now. I'll get in touch with you once we settle in where we're going. I'm sorry I had to leave like this but it's the best I could do.
Aloha,
Jayla

He whipped the legal pad across the room. It bounced off a wall rocking a framed print of a sunflower. He looked at his cut on his coffee table. He didn't even have anything big enough to store it in. He added a trip to the corner hardware store to today's agenda. First, he was going to take the nap of all naps. Once he calmed down.

His bedroom had no windows. No natural light to tell him when to wake up or fall asleep. If he had to depend on this room to set his circadian rhythm, it would never align with civilian life. And he loved his dark, cool timeless cave. He slept here on his days off. During the week, he dozed on the couch letting the rising sun wake him up.

This was a sanctuary. Yet he let his cousin sleep in his bed the first night she was here. He hadn't been in his bed in a week. He peeled off his Carhartt pants and t-shirt. Rolled between his blankets naked. He took some deep centering breaths and sunk into the mattress. On his second breath, he caught the feminine scent of Jayla. Not her minty vape but that joy and despair she carried around with her.

His thoughts clearing with every breath he lost conscious thought but still pined for his cousin.

SEVENTEEN

WHEN DR. RHINEY OPENED her office door to let him in Monday morning she was caught off guard. She said, "You shaved."

He touched his chin out of habit. Felt his large calcified jawbone. His therapist smiled and not out of pity. He welcomed her sentiment. She held a manila file folder that contained her notes on him and his sessions to her chest. He had finally dumbfounded her.

"May I come in?"

She nodded and made room for him to pass through her door. "Most certainly come in."

He sat in the oversize chair in the corner under a lamp that had soft light. Dr. Rhiney sat across from him in her ergonomic office chair. She crossed her legs and opened the file folder.

"Being sick has agreed with you."

He folded his hands in his lap. "It really swept me off my feet. But I'm feeling better."

She asked a question she had never broached before. "Can you take your glasses off for me Daniel? Just this once."

Any other time he would have balked. The time spent with Jayla and their adventure had brought him some confidence if not peace. He slowly slid his glasses off and held his head up high. Bearing himself to her. They looked at each other in the eyes without any barrier for the first time. He didn't feel judged and she didn't betray any emotion.

"Thank you. You can put them back on if you wish."

He left his glasses in his lap. "I'll wait till I leave."

"Your prerogative. What would you like to talk about today?" She jotted some notes in her folder with her fountain pen.

"I'm getting a car. I mean I've finally saved up enough money to buy one."

She perked up. "What kind of car are you going to get?"

"Something used. I still need to check around but maybe a Toyota Camry or Honda Accord. Those seem to take a lot of mileage and still be solid cars."

"A dependable automobile."

He laughed. "I guess that reveals something about me."

She touched her bottom lip with her pen. "We reveal ourselves a thousand times a day. Even when we hide our true selves, the act of concealing divulges information. If you pay attention."

"What am I divulging today?"

She frowned. "I see a mix of thoughts and emotions. You are elated but also sad. In the month in a half that we have been meeting, this is the most growth I have seen from you. What happened last week?"

She had said in the past that everything he told her inside these walls was private. As his therapist, she could not tell anyone even the court his secrets. Unless it fell within the realm of his antisocial disorder issues or he committed a crime. He knew where the line was and he knew he was going to have to dance near it now.

"While I was sick my cousin Jayla stopped by." He fiddled with his sunglasses.

"Just to visit? Dr. Rhiney asked.

He nodded. "But when she saw how sick I was she stayed and took care of me all week."

"That was kind of her. Is she from here?"

"No, she's from family in Marion County. My favorite cousin out of all of them. I hadn't seen her in ten years."

His therapist crossed her legs. "That's a long time not to see someone you cherish."

He twirled his glasses by an arm. "We were at a family reunion in Lebanon at Grandma's and Grandpa's farm. My Mom was in her cups as the Irish say. She showed her ass pretty good. Uncle Reed took ahold of her arm. She said something to him that turned him beet red and he slapped her. Hard."

He massaged the bridge of his nose. Dr. Rhiney waited

for him to catch his thoughts and proceed. He cleared his throat and said, "I didn't respond well to him striking her. She was hateful to me on good days. But she was my mother. And a woman. You aren't supposed to hit people weaker than you. You just aren't."

She said, "We've talked extensively about how you feel about bullying. How did your rage manifest itself this time?"

His eyes searched the office ceiling for answers. "I couldn't…"

"Daniel?"

He brought his gaze back to her. "I whooped his ass. Uncle Reed owned a tobacco farm. He was a grown man and country strong. I was a pale and scrawny seventeen-year-old. And I made my uncle cry. Then Uncle Bart tried to pull me off. Big mistake. Other uncles joined in and some older male cousins."

"Did they finally stop you?"

He shook his head. "Like wheat in a thresher, I cut them all down. I was getting ready to kick someone when Jayla stepped in front of me. I was breathing froth like a mad dog and she came up and hugged me. I fell into her arms and wept. That's the last hug I remember getting for years."

She asked, "What did your family do?"

"Git and never come back I heard Grandma say. Mom poured salt in the wound as we left calling all the men pussies." He sniffled a bit.

Dr. Rhiney offered him a box of tissues. He waved it off. He had cried before in her office. He wasn't ashamed of the act. But he wouldn't be shedding tears over his mother this morning. Not today.

"You never saw your extended family again?"

He shook his head. "Mom never reached out to apologize. She said those bastards want her to come home they need to beg her. No one ever did."

She said, "She blamed you as well, didn't she?"

"Yeah, I was the reason for most of her woes."

His therapist checked her notes. "I want to come back to your cousin. Jayla. Neither one of you reached out to each other in ten years?"

"We tried calling at first. That lasted for a few weeks. But neither of us had cars. She had her senior year to deal with. I dropped out and got a job. We slipped out of orbit together."

She scribbled some more notes. "That must have been a shock when she showed up at your door last week."

He smiled. "Like a scene out of your favorite movie. Jayla's something. She don't seem like much at first until she puts her shine on you."

"Her shine?"

"Yeah, shine. Doesn't stand out till she gives you her focused attention. She's pretty but so are a thousand other women. But when she connects with you, everything shines."

Dr. Rhiney fiddled with her pen. "You are describing an intoxicant."

"I suppose I am." He put his elbow on the chair's armrest and rested his chin in the palm of his hand.

"Was it all one-sided with your relationship?"

He pursed his lips. "Never thought too much about it. But she always gravitated towards me at family visits and gatherings. I would be hiding in the barn or kicking rocks in the creek by myself. Then in swoops Jayla."

"She saw something in you too."

"Maybe. Maybe light needs its shadow." He sat up straight.

"You complimented each other." More notes were scribbled down.

He pointed at her. "Yeah, we were turbo-boosted. Our tongues were sharper. Our actions bolder."

"Did that take a lot of energy to maintain? What I'm asking is, was there burnout from this turbo-boosted relationship?"

"Burnout? I mean as a kid when I left Jayla and the country, city life was dull. I hated school. No friends. Mom was a handful. You tell me was that burnout or just my regular life sucked compared to hanging out with my cousin?"

"Touché. Describe last week's visit for me?"

He relaxed and leaned back. "I almost forgot I was sick. She caught me up on what she had been doing. Which was a lot. Then my turn to tell her about my time without her. Which was a little."

"Did you stay inside all week?"

He tried to act sheepish. "I can't lie Dr. Rhiney. I felt much better halfway through the week but I wanted to spend time with Jayla. This won't get me in trouble with the Zoo will it?"

She smiled. "I doubt they will ever find out. What did you both do while playing hooky?"

He spread his hands wide. "Everything two broke cousins could do. We had adventures."

His therapist wound her pen for him to continue. "Such as?"

"She never came to the city when we were kids. Well, not to visit me. We took her car down to the waterfront by the Ohio River. Let her see the biggest creek in Kentucky. I had to grab her before she dove in."

She said, "Jayla sounds impulsive."

He nodded. "And how. We went to George Rogers Clark Park and played tennis without any rackets or balls. People thought we were nuts. Even went to Oskars for a couple of drinks one night. She's the one that got me thinking of buying a car."

Dr. Rhiney smiled. "You were out in public interacting with others a lot last week. More than usual. How did you feel with so many eyes on you?"

"I didn't give it much thought. I just ran the town with my cousin."

"There were no incidents that triggered you?"

He said, "At Oskars, there were these drunk fellas that were loud and talking about me. I used the breathing techniques you taught me. Kept my cool. Thanks to you."

She smiled some more. "Glad the breathing exercises helped."

"Wasn't just that. I kept returning to what you've told me. I can't control what others do but I can control how

I respond. Don't let people push my buttons. I'm not their robot."

"Once again I'm glad I could help. But you are doing the hard work out there, Daniel. If you can apply it to your everyday life and it brings value, that's all one can hope for," his therapist said.

"It did help. A lot last week." He winced.

"I thought there was only that one incident?"

"There was but with my cousin around I had a lot of things to process."

She made some more notes. "I see."

"She pushed me a little. Made me question my purpose in life. It's odd having someone believe in you." He massaged the back of his neck. It must be close for his session to be over.

"Faith can be a powerful motivator. But the strongest faith comes from inside you."

He said, "She gave me a boost like she always had. I just never knew what was missing until she brought her shine back."

"I'm glad your cousin could bring out such positive thoughts and energy from you. But doesn't this prove that this capability was in you all the time? Your cousin isn't the only one to shine. You are doing it at this moment." She had raised her pen and file folder while she said these words to him.

He bowed his head. "I suppose."

"No humility needed." She put her file folder back on her folded knee. "Is your cousin still in town?"

"No, she's gone. The real reason for her visit was to tie up loose ends."

She asked, "Loose ends?"

"Jayla is moving out of the country. She and a friend have a business opportunity up north in Canada."

"She came to tell you goodbye." She frowned.

"Yeah, but she said aloha." He smiled his big picket fence teeth thinking of Jayla free from her troubles.

"And you're okay with that?"

He looked at the wall clock. "I think our time is up Dr. Rhiney."

She checked her watch. "Yes, I forgot to set my timer when you surprised me this morning."

He got up from his chair and opened the door. "Thanks, Dr. Rhiney see you next week."

She uncrossed her legs and spun her chair to face him. "Next week we can talk about your missing beard."

He laughed and waved goodbye as he walked out.

FIVE
MONTHS
LATER

EIGHTEEN

DANIEL DROVE HIS HONDA back from the grocery store on the second coldest day of February. Yesterday was the coldest. He was grateful for his car that kept him from schlepping in the dirty snow-filled sidewalks and TARC buses filled with sick passengers. He took his time but chose this slate blue 2012 Civic with seventy thousand miles on it. A bargain at nine thousand eight hundred dollars.

It was the only real money he had spent from his take in the cockfighting heist. And a new heavy bag. The rest of the cash was sealed in heavy waterproof plastic and black garbage bags. He removed the stuffing from his old heavy bag and hid the money in there. The old bag sat in the corner of his workout area. The worn bag covered in duct tape would be the last place someone would look.

The money sat in its hiding place until he could think of something better to do with it or the guilt made him do something else. Something stupid. He earned his day-to-day money the old-fashioned way by working two jobs. The Zoo was seasonal and his hours got cut dramatically in the winter months. He picked up a job in late November with Target. The stock department held him over till the start of January then they laid everyone off after the Christmas rush.

He hustled and got a job down the street on Goss Avenue being a bar back at Four Pegs Lounge. His hard work got him an extra gig cooking in the kitchen. He was able to save money on food by supplementing some meals. And Miguel the head cook would give him old produce to take home a few times. They asked him to bartend but he passed. He felt under control of his anger but he didn't feel like pressing his luck by dealing with the drunken public nightly.

Life was better after his adventure with Jayla. He couldn't deny that. Two more months and his probation would be over. He didn't flame up every time someone stared or talked down to him anymore. He walked taller and looked people in the eye when he talked to them. His beard was even back. Not as bushy but it would do.

There was a weight he shouldered. All that money. It was too much for him. He wasn't the kind of guy who was supposed to have a small fortune. A question niggled at the back of his brain whenever he was deep frying someone's truffle fries at Four Pegs or cleaning the giraffe's pen. Is someone coming for him? If someone had stolen that amount of money from him, he would hunt them down.

The other shoe hadn't dropped yet. There was nothing to tie him to the crime but Jayla and Meg. They were in Canada. Archie would never go to the straight law and there was only so much his crooked cops could find out. He was a ghost to them. Some strange tweaker friend of Jayla's. He should feel free and clear. Should.

He had always felt people watching him since he looked so odd. Now vigilance needed to be maintained for the foreseeable future. He changed his travel patterns. He watched for men with bad intentions in their eyes. Cars with out-of-town plates. It was why he circled his block now looking for strange cars. Most had snow piled on them. Only one was dirty but clear of snow. A massive Yukon Denali with Illinois plates. The perfect vehicle to haul big murdering thugs from the Kentucky Fried Mafia.

As he passed by, he could see it was empty. No goons waiting for his appearance. He shook off his imagination and parked in front of Ms. Elwood's gray stone house with a white metal porch railing. He got out to unload his groceries for the week. The cold air licked the only exposed area on his face his cheeks. Three overflowing plastic bags in each hand and one in his mouth. He didn't want to make another trip to his car on this frozen Sunday.

At the rear door leading to his basement apartment, he set the bags down on the patio table. The small concrete patio was a nice place to kick up your feet and drink a beer in three out of the four seasons. Now it was just another place to shovel snow off. He took his glove off to fish the key out of his pocket. His fingers shivered a bit getting the key into the icy doorknob.

He flung the door open in a hurry, went to sweep up his grocery bags, and hustle inside to his warm place. A husky voice asked, "Need a hand with those bags?"

He darted inside his door for protection leaving his bags outside. He jutted his head out quickly in the direction of the voice. He thought he saw. No, that couldn't be. He stepped back outside into the cold windless day. Meg leaned against the stone exterior wearing a denim jacket and a watch cap for warmth.

He waved his arms directing her to his door. "Get in the house for you freeze."

She stepped through the snow in the yard with a limp. Her gift from Archie's beatdown. Her tennis shoes getting soaked cold he bet. She helped him carry his bags in. She didn't shiver or bitch about the cold. Didn't hug herself for warmth or blow hot air into her gloveless hands. Tough as nails Meg.

"You don't always have to be the baddest ass on the planet." He placed the bags on his kitchenette counter. He got two mugs out of the cupboard and a jar of store-brand instant coffee.

"You want some hot coffee?"

She shook her head. "I could go for a Yoohoo."

He laughed and put one mug back. "In the fridge. Help yourself."

He heard the fridge door open as he microwaved his

coffee. He put away a few items from his grocery bags. The microwave dinged and he took out the coffee. It tasted like ground bark but it was hot. He doubled up on the sugar, stuck the spoon in his mouth, and walked over to the fridge for some two-percent milk to cut the bitterness. Meg stood next to it not drinking her favorite chocolate beverage.

"Aren't you going to ask where your cousin is?"

He stirred the coffee in his mug. "I figured you would get to it. Only thing we have between us."

A huge grin. "Now Danny boy, didn't we have that moment shooting guns at Aunt Kelly's?"

He blushed. "What kind of trouble is she in now?"

No grin now. "I don't know."

"What's that even mean?"

She paced his small apartment. "She left. In the middle of the night while I was asleep."

"She does like an Irish goodbye." He took his bad but hot coffee with him to the couch.

"She's coming back asshole. At least her note said she was."

She tucked some hair behind her ears. It had grown shaggy since he last saw her in September. Shaggy for Meg.

"I think you two can handle your relationship without me."

She slunk over in front of the couch and looked down at him. "I can't go back alone. I'm scared okay?"

"Go back where? Is she in Marion?"

Meg hugged herself so tight she seemed to compress

her mass. Shrinking away before his eyes. "That's what the note said."

He stood up and shouted, "What else did the note say?"

She turned her back on him and murmured. He rounded his coffee table to confront her. Grasping her by her broad shoulders, he forced her to look at him.

"What aren't you telling me?"

Her eyes sought the sky but his ceiling would have to do. "The note said she was going back to Marion to get Tommy and come back home to me."

He said, "I don't. Who is Tommy?"

She tried to pull away but he held her tighter. She darted her tearing eyes about his exposed basement ceiling. "I promised Jayla."

"Who is Tommy, dammit?"

"Remember the little boy at Archie's?"

"Yeah. Archie had him on his desk and then his trashy mom took him out of the office. I remember." He loosened his grip a little. He could feel her strength returning as she let loose her secrets.

"She wasn't his Mom. Just Archie's trashy girlfriend."

He dropped his hands from her shoulders. "Tommy is Jayla's son."

Meg nodded. "We were supposed to go pick him up together when all the dust settled and Archie was kicked off his throne at the Bluegrass Sports Club. Carl kept her up to speed on what was happening. But then Carl stopped answering his phone."

"So Jayala ditched you and went back to Marion to get her son."

She slapped her thighs. "We were going to head down together. I kept making excuses. Putting it off till Spring. Whatever."

He knew but he said it anyway. "You're scared."

"I can't forget what they did to me. My body won't. And Archie's guys were brutal. I can't imagine how bad Johnny Mudd's guys are if they kicked Archie and his guys to the curb?"

She made sense. He said, "How long has she been gone?"

She held up three trembling fingers.

"Three days ain't so bad. Let me get my stuff and we'll get on our way." He turned to go to his bedroom and pack.

"Weeks." She called out behind him. "Three weeks. Almost four."

He froze and hung his head. "Meg."

"I know. I know. What are we going to do?"

He pivoted around and said, "We're going to get Jayla and her boy."

"What about Johnny Mudd and the KFM?" She was starting to tear up.

"What about Jayla? What about an innocent little boy caught up in this shit?" He clenched his fists. Could feel that old heat flushing up to his neck. Meg saw it in his posture.

"Okay. Save that rage, we'll need it when we ride into Marion."

He counted his breaths and when he got to his second count of ten, he unclenched his hands. "You have to be all in Meg. I'll do this alone if I have to but I could use your help. What they did to you. If you can't go just say so now."

She wiped her tears away. "She needs me."

He raised his voice, "That ain't an answer."

That got her ire up. "You're riding shotgun."

He slapped her on her arm and walked over to his old heavy bag on the floor. "I'm going to grab a couple of things and we'll roll."

"No offense to your tactical genius but why are you packing a used punching bag?"

He squatted down by the bag and flicked open his pocket knife. He cut through the duct tape he wrapped around the bag over four months ago. Standing up he showed her a plastic-wrapped bag of his money.

"Get my duffel bag out of the closet and load up the money while I pack. We may need this to barter for Jayla and Tommy."

She took the money bag from him. "You didn't spend it?"

"I got a car. Rest is all there."

"You are one strange dude, Daniel."

"I never needed much so I never wanted much." He went to his bedroom to pack knowing that was a lie he told himself.

NINETEEN

DANIEL WASN'T A DETECTIVE. They made it to Marion County around dusk and he still hadn't figured out how to locate his cousin. Just drive around town and country till they spotted her. He made a list in his head. Check with family first. Aunt Kelly's place. Find Carl Donger. Go to the Bluegrass Sports Club. Talk with Archie. Burn the club to the ground. It was a flexible list.

Meg had shown him her small arsenal hidden in the Denali's rear cargo space floor. All those guns made him uncomfortable but they were just tools for extracting information as a dentist did teeth. The information they would need to find and get Jayla out of here. Every last bullet would be used if Archie or Johnny Mudd's guys got in his way.

For all his bravado, he would rather not have a Shootout at the OK Corral. He stuck to his list. They drove to Filiatreau Road. It was a hard left in Lebanon and ten miles of snow-covered fields to the big metal mailbox that said The Durands on it. Grandma would hear them coming down the mile-long gravel road. Gravel roads are the country's early warning system.

And if the heavy SUV on her gravel driveway failed, there was always a scroungy mutt or four to bark at them when they reached the limestone farmhouse. He didn't see his favorite dog Snapper in the pack. Ten years was a long time He was either dead or too tired to run out in the cold and bark at strangers.

Meg parked the car careful not to hit any of the dogs. "Damn they're a loud bunch. Think they bite."

"No, but she might." He pointed up the front door where an older woman could be seen.

Meg whistled. "May Durand. Jayla said she was a handful."

He opened his door. "Put your hat on and let's go. She don't like to be kept waiting."

Jayla got out and headed towards the front door. He swung his head to his right and said, "We go in around back. Where the mudroom is."

Meg limped around to him. "Then why didn't we park closer to the back."

"Because this is where we park."

"We who?"

"Family." He led her to the mudroom door. It was an old swing door and he held it for her so it didn't come back and pop her.

"I'm not family." She tentatively entered.

"No, and she'll point that out once we're inside." He let the door shut when he followed her inside.

The mudroom was added to the hundred-year-old farmhouse sometime in the early fifties. It didn't look out of place. The dark wood had aged and worn itself right into the limestone wall. This was a gathering place for tools, outdoor gear, and wet boots to be kept from the interior of the main house. He peeled off his tennis shoes.

Meg said, "I ain't taking off my boots. My socks will get wet."

He shrugged. "Take them off or get hit in the ear with a wooden spoon. Your choice."

"I didn't see Jayla at the door with your grandma. Still think she's here?"

"I don't know. But we all turn to family in times of trouble."

"You turn to your Mom?"

"She's the trouble you turn from." He walked up the two peeling linoleum steps and opened the inner house door.

He stepped into his yesteryear. A gigantic kitchen with high ceilings. A blocky pinewood dining table that could seat twelve healthy farm boys. And used to squeeze in more than that on Sunday dinners. There were nicks and cigarette burns on the knotty pine surface. Every once in a while, Grandma would rub linseed oil on it. He ran his fingers over it remembering.

"You must be looking for Jayla." Grandma came in from the darkened living room.

Meg stood in the door frame. Wary to enter. She said, "Is she here?"

His Grandma stood barely over five feet tall. Her body was as stout as the barrel of pork crackling they passed in the mudroom. The warmth of her smile welcomed him many a time when he felt less than normal. And when she gave you her hardness in her eyes, you knew not to mess around with Grandma Durand. She inspected Meg like a piece of kindling to be snapped and burned.

She turned her attention back to him. "Some other people been looking."

"Grandma, this is Meg. Friend of Jayla's."

"If you say so." She went to the white stove that had always been in the house. A pot was boiling on it.

"You making sweat tea?" He took off his jacket and placed it around the kitchen chair closest to him.

"I am. There is some leftover chicken in the fridge if you want to make a plate. I'll heat up the oven and warm up some biscuits." His Grandma pulled the towel off some hard biscuits in a bowl on the counter.

Meg finally entered the kitchen. "Where is Jayla?"

He went over to her and guided her towards an empty chair at the table. "Have a seat. Best biscuits in Kentucky."

"She's a big'un. Better get some ham too." She put the biscuits on a beat-up sheet pan and into the hot oven.

He used his body to shield his conversation with Meg and whispered, "Just settle down and enjoy the food. She'll tell us in good time."

She pushed him back a little. "I ain't here to mollycoddle some old lady. Time is…ow!"

Grandma held a long wooden spoon cocked back by her shoulder. "Call me old again and you won't be hearing out of your right ear for two days."

Meg rubbed her left ear. "Okay. Okay. No mas."

"And lay off that Spanish gibberish. Get enough of that from Gilberto and Cisco." She went back to the stove and stirred the boiling tea with the wooden spoon.

He got the sliced country ham out of the refrigerator. "Who are Gilberto and Cisco?"

"They help your Uncle Edgar with the farm since your Grandpa died and no one else wanted to help."

He lowered his head. "Sorry about Grandpa."

She came over and kissed him on his bearded cheek. "You paid your respects at the funeral. Know it wasn't easy showing up after all.. well after all. At least you came."

"I'm sure Mom wanted to come."

"You don't have to make excuses for her. She is what she is. She's still a Durand but she left the family before you were born."

She got a cranberry Tupperware tea pitcher out of the kitchen cabinet. Vintage would be the kind word for it. She poured the steeping hot tea into the pitcher. After she pulled a couple of bags that had fallen into it out, she pulled a heavy ceramic crock over. Three coffee cups full of granulated sugar went into the tea pitcher. Grandma stirred it roughly and put the airtight lid back on.

Daniel had placed two jelly glasses on the table with ice. Grandma put the pitcher of tea on the table and went back to get her warmed-up biscuits. Meg crossed and uncrossed her arms expressing her irritation. He poured her a glass of sweet tea.

"It's not Yoohoo but give it a go."

"Quit handling me. I'm not some kid at the grownups table." She took a sip from her glass anyway. Her lips pursed after a taste.

"Did you lose a tooth?" He took a big drink himself.

"I think I lost all of them. Lordy, that's sweet. Mrs. Durand, are you part hummingbird?"

His Grandma placed the biscuits wrapped in a towel on the table and had a seat. "I have been accused of being an agent of the Tooth Fairy once or twice. Have a biscuit, kids."

She watched them eat a couple of biscuits. Grandma even had one with a slice of salty ham herself. She didn't drink the sweet tea. She had her white porcelain bottomless mug that was filled with chicory coffee. All he ever saw her drink. Summer or winter. Night or day. His Grandma was an immortal being like he read about in stolen encyclopedias from the school library.

"Best biscuits in Kentucky? Best biscuits in America, I say." Meg finished off her crumbly biscuit and reached for another one.

Grandma eyed her over her mug. "Sell it somewhere else Sally."

"Ma'am?"

Grandma put her right hand on the wooden spoon in her apron pocket. Meg dropped the biscuit back on the plate and covered her ear. "Enough with the flattery. Ask your questions."

He said, "Sorry Grandma. We just need to find Jayla."

She sipped some of her coffee. "Maybe she don't want to be found?"

Meg tapped the table. "She was here. I knew it."

"Young lady what you know wouldn't fit between two halves of my biscuit."

He said, "She's from Ohio."

"They got manners up north. No, this one is full of pride. You know what the Lord says about that."

Meg pushed her plate away. "Didn't come here for bible lectures or biscuits or tea that will melt your teeth. Jayla's in trouble. And I'll kick every ass in this county till I find her."

Grandma grinned a little before she sipped her coffee. "I see why Jayla likes you. You're a fun fire to poke."

"We really are trying to help Jayla. Did she visit in the last three weeks?" he asked.

She put her mug down and tented her fingers. "Said she was looking for her mama. Your Aunt Shelly done moved again."

"She's at Aunt Shelly's then?"

"Don't know. She said she was looking for her mama but I told her she could stay with me if she needed to. I thought we ironed it out but in the morning she was gone."

Meg said, "Girl has a slipping away problem."

He laid his hand over his grandmother's on the table. "Do you think she went to her Mom's place after all?

She tsked. "Shelly isn't as bad as your mama Daniel but

she strolls the same neighborhood. No, I think Jayla was here for someone else but wouldn't tell me. Something you two know."

He pulled his hand back slowly. Grandma had a built-in shit detector better than any FBI interrogator. "Not my secret to share Grandma."

She looked at Meg. "Anything you can add?"

"Not my secret either."

Grandma sat up straighter. "Couple of myna birds you are. Is she in danger?"

Meg's gaze fell to her plate filled with biscuit crumbs. Daniel nodded.

"You all did some bad things," she said. It wasn't a question.

"We did but we were free and clear. I mean I thought we were. Jayla didn't tell me everything."

Grandma got up and went over to the kitchen counter and got out a pack of generic unfiltered cigarettes. She hit the pack against her wrist and took out one cigarette. She struck a wooden match with her thumbnail and lit the tobacco. After she waved the match out, she came back to the table.

She savored her lone cigarette. "You going to save Jayla like you used to when you were kids?"

"Yes ma'am."

She watched the smoke swirl to the ceiling. "Do you have it in you, son?"

"If she doesn't come back, I'm not coming back," he said.

"You all in too girlie?"

Meg said, "I can't live without her Mrs. Durand."

Grandma sighed. "Call me May. You two can rest here while you look for Jayla."

Meg stood up. "I'll fetch our stuff out of the truck."

"Un uh. You can sleep here after you find her. Don't care if it takes all night."

Meg smiled. "Yes ma'am."

He gathered his coat off the chair and gave his Grandma a kiss goodbye on the cheek. "We'll get her back."

She patted his cheek. "You know where to look?"

"I got a list."

"Archie Mudd the first name on it?"

"Top of the list, Grandma."

She got a pad of paper and a pencil off the table. They used it to keep the score of Buck Pitch. Only card game they played. She scribbled on the notepad. "You're going to need his address. I hear he isn't at his club no more."

He raised his eyebrows but accepted the piece of paper. "You know why?"

"Johnny Mudd took over is all I heard. Think you can find Archie's place with your doohickey phone."

He showed the note to Meg and she plugged in the address to the GPS app on her phone. "Got it, let's go."

Meg hustled out the door. He walked slower waving goodbye to his grandmother but followed her out into the dark.

TWENTY

ON THE DRIVE TO ARCHIE'S PLACE between the GPS navigational voice telling them to bear left or in two miles take a right, Meg said, "I don't know why Jayla didn't leave and take Tommy to your Grandma's when things got bad?"

"Then she never would have met you." He scratched his whiskered chin.

She tightened her grip on the steering wheel. "That might not have been a bad thing."

"Someone once told me that you can't keep looking behind to see what's chasing you. You keep your eyes forward on what you're chasing."

"Your therapist tell you that?"

He inspected his cuticles. "Maybe. Might have heard Ric Flair say it."

She said, "I think it was your therapist."

"Really? Couldn't be the Nature Boy?"

"If it was Flair, you would have had to the 'wooooo' at the end. You didn't do the 'wooooo' hence Ric Flair didn't say it."

He smirked. "I did not have sexual relations with that woman. Wooooo!"

"Four score and seven years ago. Wooooo!" she said.

"Life is like a bowl of chocolates. Wooooo!"

They were both laughing pretty hard. He caught her giving him a look. So he asked, "What?"

"Nothing. It's just nice. I know aren't my biggest fan."

"I wouldn't take it personally Meg. Just my nature to throw up a wall pretty fast."

"Yeah, you do have that ugly chip on your shoulder."

He bristled at that comment. "I don't have a chip on my…."

"Yeah, you do. Ain't no reason either. Plenty of homely people out there. You don't hear about them picking fights every time somebody looks at them funny."

He crossed his arms. "I recall why I'm not your biggest fan."

She reached over and tugged on his sleeve. "You're not easy on the eyes. I'm loud and obnoxious. We all have our crosses to bear."

He brushed her off. "Hands on the wheel."

"We're like a brother and sister the way we fight."

He said, "We aren't even friends. How the hell did you leap to siblings?"

"Why I said this was nice. I've never had a brother."

"I forgot you were a foster kid. Didn't you have foster brothers or sisters?"

"If you mean rivals, yes. But they were never family."

He felt a little embarrassed. "That's nice to hear."

She slapped him hard across his chest. A solid whap. "I said like a brother. We aren't family until I marry that cousin of yours."

The voice said they were at their destination on Tyler Road. Meg rolled to a stop on the side of the road. A rusty mailbox sat at the end of a gravel driveway that had most of the numbers of the address. The driveway winded back into a small forest. Most of the trees were leafless but there were some spruce and other evergreens to block their line of sight to Archie's house. They couldn't even see any lights in the distance.

"We're just going to walk into the lion's den and get her?"

He said, "We'll use the element of surprise."

"They'll be surprised when the pee comes down my pants leg."

He pulled out his cell phone and fake dialed a number then put it to his ear. "Hello. Yes, I'm looking for the meanest bitch I ever met. Her name was Meg. Has anyone seen her?"

"Asshole." She put the SUV back into gear and pulled into the driveway. The Denali rolled over the gravel so smoothly it might as well have been paved asphalt. It was only a little after nine in the evening but the sun in February set early.

She turned the headlights off and slowly found her way with just the running lights. Still might attract attention but wouldn't announce their approach as brightly. They came around a bend and the house rested in a clearing. A modern two-story house with mixed red brick lit up by exterior mounted lights. A large two-car garage was connected to the house with a covered walkway. As you got closer to the house part of the driveway was paved with concrete.

She backed the SUV up a bit off to the side of the road as close to the tree line as she could get. All the lights were turned off now. She kept the Denali running with its throttled purr. Daniel stared at the house for a moment. "We need to go take a look. He might not be there."

"You think?"

He opened the door and got out. "You stay here. I'll signal you to pull up if he's here."

"Wait a sec. What kind of signal?"

"I'm not going to shoot a flare gun off. Just keep your eyes open."

"Speaking of guns. You better take something with you." She motioned with her head to the back of the SUV.

He shut the door as quietly as he could and went to the rear of the Denali. She had popped the rear door and he opened it the rest of the way. He lifted open her rear hatch and looked at the guns in the oilcloth.

"Take the Glock. It's like the one you had on our last adventure."

He chose the handgun she said and put it in his coat pocket. "I'm just going to see if he's there. Then I'll signal you to pull up and we'll both go in together."

He shut the rear door and hurried across the driveway to the left. This side of the forest would give him protection up to the house. It gave him options instead of walking up a clearing and ringing the doorbell. He felt watched the whole time he snuck up the two hundred yards to the back corner of the garage. He poked around the corner and a light came on. He fell on his ass and crab-walked back behind the garage.

He started to take off running but no one came out, no noises or movement, and the light went off. It was a motion sensor. He crept back around the corner not caring when the light came back on. He followed the outside of the covered walkway. An obstacle course of shrubs and other landscaping in the back led to an expansive patio deck. One entrance into the house from the deck was a large double door. He looked inside while checking the slide. It was locked. The only lights he could see were from the oven clock and the refrigerator's water dispenser.

There was another door at the other end of the wide deck. He went down to inspect that one. He couldn't see any lights on at all in any window from the house. Wait. He saw some flickering blue light coming from the window just past the door he approached. The door was white without any windows or peepholes. He checked the doorknob and it turned easily. Before he went inside, he decided to look in the window with a faint blue light.

At the window, he slowly leaned in for a peek. A

widescreen TV displayed some school of fish swimming in an ocean. A nature documentary of some sort. He could just make out the British narrator speaking. Daniel also peeped two hairy legs with feet in socks kicked up on a leather ottoman. Someone lounged in a leather chair watching fish. On a table next to the chair sat a comically large bottle of Jack Daniels.

He went back to the door and put his left hand on the knob. His right hand pulled out the handgun from his coat pocket. He held the gun barrel flat against his forehead and felt the coolness of it. He put it back in his pocket but left the pocket unzipped. The door opened without a creak and he slipped in quickly in case the cold aroused whoever sat in the chair. Unfortunately, the door shut with a whump.

A man's head with messy hair rose over the leather chair's back. "Who's scare?"

Daniel reached into his pocket gripping the pistol's handle. His heart pounded but he circled wide to the side of the chair and came around to see who was watching schools of fish eaten by bigger fish. Archie spread out along the chair and ottoman in an iridescent blue bathrobe. He rested a rock glass half full of whisky on his belly. His eyes half shut searched Daniel's face for any recognition.

"I said who's scare?" His belly moved when he spoke almost spilling his whisky.

"I think you mean there. Who's there."

"Fuck you." He drank from his glass and turned his attention back to the fish on the TV.

Daniel noticed the fireplace and sidestepped to it keeping an eye on Archie. He picked up a fire poker from the stand and hid it behind his leg. He came back over and picked up the large remote sitting on the coffee table. He found the mute button and pressed it. No more British chap, no more waves lapping.

"Hey. What're you doin'? I was watching that."

Daniel whipped the metal rod of the fire poker across Archie's exposed shins. Kerack! Metal on bone. Archie howled like an alley cat. He pulled his legs up to his chair both rubbing them and protecting them. The rock glass full of whisky spilled off his lap and bounced to a stop by Daniel's feet on the hardwood floor.

"Are you one of Morale's boys?"

Daniel said, "Do I look like I'm from Mexico?"

"I can't tell with them big glasses on. Could be." He touched his shins and winced.

"Guess again." Daniel poked at the leather chair with the hook end.

"Not one of Johnny's people. He wouldn't kill family. Hurt, maim, exile but no killing."

Daniel looked around at the humongous TV than at all the luxurious furniture in the expansive house. He swept the poker around in the air. "This doesn't quite look like you're in exile to me."

"He cut me off at the goddamn knees. Threw me out of my club. My club!"

Daniel prodded the leather chair again with the metal poker. "And why did your brother kick you out?"

He reached over and grabbed the bottle of Jack Daniels

by the neck. "That bitch stole everyone's money! Johnny made me pay it all back out of my pocket. But I think he kept it for himself. Didn't pay Morales or any of the betters back."

"Is that why you think I'm from El Mencho?"

"Yeah, those beaners don't mess around. Who gives a fuck if I can pay the mortgage? I'm a dead man anyway." Archie reached out towards the floor. "Can I get that glass back?"

Daniel swung the poker into the rock glass like Tiger Woods teeing off on the 18th hole. It slid across the wood floor and cracked into the natural rock fireplace but it didn't shatter.

Archie said, "That was rude."

Daniel swung the poker in a fierce arc catching Archies socked toes. There was a crunching sound almost like Cheetos being eaten. Archie cried out pitching the liquor bottle over his head and clutched his left foot.

"Why? Why are you hurting me? I don't have any more money? My cars are all gone. You want my TV? Take it!"

Daniel hit the floor hard with the poker. He dragged it in the wood hard leaving massive gouges on the floor between him and Archie. "I don't want any of that shit. I want you to pay attention."

"Just tell me what you want you ugly son of a bitch?" He cried tears but out of pain or anger or resignation, Daniel couldn't surmise.

"Where is Jayla?"

"Jayla?"

"You know Jayla. The bitch that stole all your money?" Daniel cocked back the poker.

Archie held his hands. "Hold it! Hold it. Jayla isn't here. Johnny has her."

Daniel felt the heat flushing up to his back into his neck in shoulders. He used the heat in his muscles to swing the poker into Archies outstretched palms. A thick whud. Archie recoiled back into his chair with a whine.

"I don't deserve this," he whimpered.

"I'm going to break every bone on your ever-loving body then heat this poker and shove it up your ass. Quit messing around and tell me where Jayla is."

Through tears of pain this time, Archie said, "At Johnny's farm most likely. Give me a piece of paper and I'll write down the address."

Daniel shook his head. "Not good enough. You're going to show me."

"Show you? Show you? Johnny will kill me if I walk in his door with you."

He patted the poker neck in his palm. "I thought he didn't kill family?"

"I'm a half-brother." Archie pleaded, "I can barely stand."

"You'll dance if I tell you. Now get up. We're leaving."

"Jesus, can I at least put shoes on for Christ's sake?"

Daniel saw some gore-tex boots by the door she entered. He walked over, picked them up then came back and tossed them in Archie's lap. "Lace them up and let's go."

"Alright. Alright." Archie struggled to put on the boots

one-handed but he got them on. He went to stand up and had to favor his right foot.

"Take us out the front door," said Daniel.

Archie followed orders and led them out limping all the way. He held his injured left hand close to his chest. As they walked through his house, Daniel released some anger by swiping at vases and framed pictures with the poker. Each crash and breaking glass made Archie's shoulders clench. They made it to the front door and Daniel turned on all the porch lights. He swung the door wide open then pushed his hostage out into the cold February night.

"Christ it's freezing." Archie clutched at his robe.

Daniel stood in the light and waved the poker high in the air towards Meg waiting in her Tahoe. The SUV growled to life and she drove up towards the circle drive in front of the house.

He looked over his shoulder and asked, "Who is Jayla to you?"

"You answer questions. You don't ask them."

"Okay, Buffalo Bill. I'll put the lotion on my skin."

Meg parked the SUV and got out to meet them at the steps. As she approached, she said, "Do we need him conscious?"

Daniel nodded his head. "Sorry, he's got to show us the way."

Archie spun his head back and forth between them. "What's she sayi...uff!"

She threw a punch from downtown Peoria into Archie's stomach. Her fist slipped right between the robes and sunk into his soft belly. He lurched over the porch rail and threw up into the icy grass. Stomach acid and Tennessee whisky perfumed the air. He swung back up awkwardly and held onto the rail half sliding and stumbling down the porch steps. At the bottom, he fell onto his back on the cold lawn.

Meg took two steps over to the prone man and punted into his ribs with her boot. Archie tried to roll and cover so she kicked him in his lower back. He remained in the fetal position crying and shaking. Daniel walked over stood next to her and stared down at him. Archie looked back with his right eye. It wasn't exactly clear but his left eyelid didn't seem to want to open. His right eye did widen and he said, "Your Jayla's dyke." Then he farted and passed out.

Daniel jabbed him with the fire poker. Archie didn't stir. "Dammit. We needed him awake."

She said, "What did you find out?"

"He said his brother Johnny has Jayla."

"Johnny Mudd? The Don of the Kentucky Fried Mafia. Swell."

"Except he has to show us because his farm doesn't show right on the GPS app. And now he's out." He pointed the poker at the snoring drunk to emphasize his point.

"He would have blacked out with or without or help tonight. It smells like he drank half his body weight in corn liquor."

He flipped the poker over into the grass and went around to Archie's head and shoulders. "Grab his feet."

"I don't want him stinking up my ride."

"Pick up…We need him to find Jayla."

"Let me open the damn door." She opened the rear passenger door then moved to the end of Archie's feet murmuring under her breath.

"What's that?"

She got a grip on his feet. "I said that was some great signal. Coming out the front door with a half-naked man swinging a poker."

"On the count of three. One, two, three."

They hoisted him up in unison. The deadweight of his blacked-out body was significant but they took quick tiny steps and got him to the open door. He slid Archie's upper torso onto the seat. He ran around to the other side and reached in grabbing the robe's collar and pulled the drunk idiot in as Meg steadied his feet. She slammed the door shut.

As she got behind the steering wheel, she said, "You're cleaning his puke up when it happens."

He got in his side of the Tahoe and looked back over the seat at their guest slash hostage. "I'll clean up his mess. How long do you think he will be out?"

"I had a foster mother who would blackout from drinking but still clean the house or cook dinner. Mind you this was three o'clock in the morning."

"So, sometime between now and dawn?"

"Drinking is an art, not a science. What did you want from me?"

He rolled his shoulders. The adrenaline from all the violence he inflicted on Archie was dumping. "Let's find an all-night diner by the highway and see if some food will sober him up."

She put the SUV in drive and drove out of the circle to the main drive. "I like your plans. Have that improv feel to them."

Daniel didn't disagree. He recalled that famous science fiction writer's quote about jumping off the cliff and building your wings on the way down. That's how he's felt since Jayla walked back into his life five months ago and he helped her rob a cockfighting championship. He looked up out of his window at the stars thinking the feeling couldn't last forever.

TWENTY-ONE

THEY FOUND A TWENTY-FOUR-HOUR Huddle House open on Main St in Lebanon. Meg got twitchy and it wasn't just that they had a kidnapped unconscious man in the SUV. The Marion County Detention Center was about a football field length away from the local chain diner. Daniel felt kind of out in the open himself. He got out and went inside for coffee and some hot starchy grub like a deer approaching a salt lick left out by a hunter.

The bell over the door dinged and caught his attention. When he corrected his line of sight, he locked eyes with a waitress. She had been dealt with the ugly card he received himself from that fickle dealer Fate. They nodded in recognition. As he walked over to place his carryout order, he noticed a large round fellow wearing a uniform tapping the ash off his cigarette into a cheap gold aluminum ashtray. His shoulder patch read Marion County Corrections.

Two waitresses and the correction officer were the only company in the bright diner. He could smell greasy bacon sizzling and hear a metal spatula sliding on a flat grill coming from behind a swing door with a round window on it. Daniel imagined a short-order cook dressed in white with grease stains and a cigarette dangling from his lips in the back kitchen. The waitress he made eye contact with earlier came over to the counter.

"What can I get for you?"

He said, "Four large coffees."

"Black?"

"Two black. The other two with plenty of sugar and cream please."

She wrote down his order on a pad. "Anything to eat?"

He glanced down at the guard. The heavy fellow listed a bit. Either drunk or sleepy. Maybe both. "You all have ham and egg biscuits?"

"We sure do, hon. How many you want?"

"Three biscuits. And hash brown patties if you have them?"

"We got hash browns but not in patty form. They're delish." She poked his hand with the eraser end of his pencil.

"They are?" Was she flirting with him? Waitresses usually ignored him. One he was unattractive and two he was poor.

"Sometimes all I eat all week are the hash browns. God as my witness." She smiled and bewitched him.

"You don't care do you?" he asked.

"Care about the hash browns? They're tasty and all but I wouldn't say I was in love with them."

He touched his glasses. "I mean you don't care what others think about how you look."

She cocked her hip. "Sometimes I do. On bad days. But no, generally I don't give a damn what some nasty person thinks about me."

"Someone told me how someone treats me is not in my control. What I do about it, is in my control. Thought I was doing better."

She gave him that thousand watts smile again. "What's your name?

"Daniel."

"Well, Daniel. I don't know if you believe in a higher power or fate or any other bugaboo philosophy, but I believe we got one life to live and it's a huge waste of energy to worry about assholes. Don't you?"

He found his hand drawing near her hand on the counter. "In theory, I do. In practice, I fail a lot."

"Anger isn't a terrible emotion unless you hold onto it. Build into a rage. Rage must go somewhere. If it stays inside you, it hurts you. If you let it out, it hurts others."

Her hand seemed to be inching towards his as well. "Are you majoring in psychology?"

"I sure am. Every shift I work is a class on the human experience."

Their fingers were almost there. He laughed. "I guess that's true."

She grabbed her pad off the counter. "Let me get those biscuits and hash browns going."

She left him at the counter staring at his lonely hand on the counter so dumbfounded he had to sit down on the counter stool. He came in for food but received another type of sustenance. The other waitress a little younger than the one he talked to smiled and followed her coworker into the kitchen. He heard a little laughter come from the back.

"Molly's sharp as a tack." A voice from his left rasped.

Daniel didn't turn his head but glanced left and saw the guard looking at him. He turned his head and nodded in agreement.

"She ain't much to look at but I'd vote for her if she ran for mayor."

At the mention of her looks, Daniel tightened his fingers into fists. "I've only known her for five minutes and I would too."

Molly came back out with the other waitress tailing right behind her. Molly went left and the other girl veered right. She said, "Be a minute on your food. I'll get your coffee now."

"Thanks, Molly" he said.

The guard said, "I told him you're running for mayor Molly."

The other waitress brought a glass coffee pot over to the guard. "Tell me more about the prisoner you stopped from escaping Tony. The firebug."

The waitress topped off the guard's coffee mug and winked at Molly. Molly mouthed thank you. Tony started right in where he must have left off five years ago regaling the waitress on his heroics. Molly straightened her apron and got busy filling his coffee order. She got the fourth one filled then put them in a cardboard carrier and placed that in a white bag with the Huddle House logo.

She sat the bag in front of him on the counter. He said, "Thanks, mayor."

"Tony's so full of it. But I would be a damn good mayor if I put my mind to it."

He slid the bag to the side and put his forearms on the counter. "Is that what you want to do with your life? Get into politics."

"Sad to say but at this point in my life I'm not sure what I want to be."

He put his left elbow on the counter and rested his bearded chin in his hand. "Just testing the waters as a practicing therapist slash waitress slash philosopher?"

"Something like that. I might start roaming the country town to town working at diners at night, fighting crime in the morning." She leaned on the counter mirroring his elbow pose. "What do you do Daniel?"

"I think I'm sort of like you. I don't know what to be. Been so busy trying to stay out of sight I fell off the path."

She said, "You've lost your way in the forest."

He felt a sadness welling up in his answer. "For a long time."

"I believe you can find your way out. Your past doesn't define you."

He looked up at a clock on the wall whose hands pointed to 1:30. "Is this a zen, be present at the moment pep talk?"

She gave a cute tight lip smile and said, "Why not wring every ounce out of life while you're here?"

Before he could mull over what she said a bell dinged and a man's voice called, "Orders up."

She patted his forearm on the counter and went back through the swing door. The door was on its backward swing when Molly came back carrying another white paper bag. She put it on the counter next to his bag full of coffee.

"There you go. All set for your travel in the dead of night."

He was supposed to take the bags and leave. He had tasks to render. Ugly tasks. But still, he sat there. Unable to move. Then there was a hard knock on the glass window behind him. He looked and found Meg pressed against the window. When she got his attention, she pointed to her left wrist like it had a watch then hooked her thumb in a let's go manner.

He did a few nods to Meg letting her know he got the message then picked up his carry-out bags. Molly with a grin on her face asked, "Your friend's in a hurry."

"She's not exactly a friend."

Molly feigned surprise. "Oh?"

Even though he was holding a full bag of coffee, he managed to point a finger. "No. No oh's. She's my cousin's girlfriend. We're out looking for her. Look it's a long story and I want to tell you all about it and I want you to tell me everything about you. But now isn't the time."

She placed both hands on the counter wide and leaned over. "We have time later for all of that."

His brow furrowed. "I'm an idiot. Pretty big one in fact but I'm going to take your advice to heart. Live in the moment. I can't promise I'll be back Molly. But if I'm not, it isn't by choice."

"Need any help?"

"Lord yes but I'll have to make do with who I've got right now. Night, Molly." He should wear a cowboy hat. Tipping a ball cap doesn't have the same effect. He gathered his bags and walked towards the door.

"Night Daniel."

He turned for one last smile and went out in the cold night. Meg was waiting and he handed her the bag of coffee. She opened it, stuck her nose in, and took a big breath. She said, "Ah, sweet elixir of caffeine."

"Aren't you supposed to be in the truck watching Archie?"

"Guys so snockered Godzilla walking through Lebanon couldn't wake him up."

"Not the point."

She swept her left arm around his shoulders and pulled him close. "You were taking forever. I came to see why and what do I spy with my little eye but you flirting with the waitress. Such a cliché Daniel."

He unhooked her arm. "I was talking with Molly."

"Oooo Molly. Sounds serious. Did you tell her we have a beaten unconscious man in our truck?"

He opened the rear passenger door and got in and slammed the door. "Didn't come up."

She got in the driver's side and asked back at him, "What was that?"

"I said it didn't come up. Can we focus on finding Jayla now?"

She handed him a large coffee. "Get his ass awake and maybe we can find her."

He tried to hold Archie's face up to sip some coffee. He could see his eyes doing that rem movement under his eyelids but that was it.

"Where should I drive to while you're waking up the asshole?"

"Just find some secluded place. No cops."

"No shit Daniel." She put the SUV in reverse and backed up. He looked out the rear window and saw Molly backlit in the Huddle House. He took her advice and enjoyed the view as they left the parking lot.

The sleek black Yukon sat halfway in the middle of the Filiatreau's unmarked dirt driveway off Brian Road. He assumed it led to a house at the end but over a half-mile in and covered in a canopy of maple and oak trees they never saw any trace of a home or its residents. At two in the morning in this sleepy county, it was more than secluded. It was off any radar.

Meg munched on her ham and egg biscuit between sips from her hot coffee. She let him try to rouse Archie with coffee and some slaps to the face did nothing. He thought he saw his nose twitch when Daniel held the hash browns close to his lips. Just an involuntary reaction to the scent of fried potatoes. Nothing worked on Archie's booze snooze.

"At this rate, we'll never get to that farm. Hell, Jayla and her kid may not even be there. I just don't…"

She held onto the biscuit in her mouth, took the hand that was holding it, and tipped the coffee cup in Daniel's hand until the hot coffee poured into Archie's crotch. The sleeping man howled himself back into the waking world. He thrashed around taking hold of his burnt genitalia. Daniel grasped his robed shoulders and held him in place.

"My balls are on fire."

Daniel slapped his cheek. "Calm down. Is something on fire when it's wet?"

He let go of his crotch and felt his damp fingers. "Fair point."

"But if you don't lead us to Johnny's farm, I'm going to light your tiny dick up."

"He'll kill me."

"You said he wouldn't kill family back at the house."

Archie started to tear up. "I'm a half-brother."

"So, he'll kill half of you?"

He nodded. "And beat the other half silly. Johnny don't mess around."

Daniel put the mostly empty Styrofoam coffee cup in a side door holder. He reached his hand over the front seat towards her. "Punch in that lighter and let me see it."

She gave a wicked smile then pushed in the cigarette

lighter under the radio on the dash. The audible click in the cab made Archie flinch.

"Takes about five seconds for those coils to heat up enough to set flame to tobacco. How do you think the hairs on your balls will smell?" Daniel held up his left fist and started extending his fingers in a countdown.

"I can't" He blubbered. "Johnny."

Before Daniel's fifth digit went up the lighter popped out ready to light. Meg handed him the safe end. "Light up them balls."

He took the lighter from her and let Archie see the glowing coil. He blew on them to make them glow even brighter. "Might want to crack a window. Let the smell out."

She whirred the rear window Archie leaned against down a little. Winter air rushed into the seam. Daniel flipped the robe open revealing Archie's soaked from the coffee boxers. He moved the lighter closer to his crotch. Sweat beads popping on Archie's forehead. A combination of fear and alcohol pumping out. Daniel barely touched his cotton boxers with the hot end of the lighter and their hostage yelped.

"Okay!"

Daniel pulled back the lighter just smidge. "Okay, what?"

"I'll take you to Johnny's."

Daniel handed the lighter back to Meg and she stuck it back in the console. Archie pulled his robe back together and rubbed his red jowls. "I ain't straight."

Meg said, "Well, gosh Archie neither am I but you don't see me crying about it."

"I gotta get straight. I need some brown juice."

Daniel reached over the front seat and got a big bottle of Jack Daniels he had taken from Archie's place. He unscrewed the cap and poured a large amount into the coffee cup in the door holder. He swirled what little was left of the coffee with the added whisky then handed it to Archie. He took the offering and immediately quaffed the whole concoction down.

He held out the cup to Daniel. "Get another pour."

Daniel looked at Meg and she said, "One more then it's off to Johnny's."

"Two will do I always say."

Daniel poured once more a little less generous this time into the cup. Archie frowned at the amount but tipped it back till it was all gone. He held it up and shook out every last drop. Daniel placed the liquor bottle on the floorboard away from the drunken fool. Archie smacked his gums.

"That's as straight as you're going to get," said Daniel. "Let's go to Johnny's."

"One more toast to our doom?"

Meg tossed a ham biscuit in his lap. "Toast that biscuit and let's haul."

He unwrapped the biscuit and took a large bite. He mumbled through the crumble. Daniel stepped on his toes. He swallowed his biscuit and said, "What is this dirt road off of?"

"Meg said, "Filiatreau Way."

"That's fine. Head back to it and hang a left. We get to Hearth Road and I can find the way." He took another ample bite on his biscuit. "Damn, Huddle House has the best biscuits. Ugly waitresses but great food."

Daniel stomped on his toes again much harder than last time. Archie yelled, "Mothertrucker! Why do you keep hurting me?"

Daniel couldn't answer that. He just had a bottomless pit of pain he wanted to give Archie. He hoped he could be different. That maybe Molly from Huddle House saw something inside him that wasn't as ugly as his outside. But he didn't think his pit would ever be empty from the hurt.

Meg turned the SUV around and drove them out of there towards the main road. She turned the radio on and found some bland new country song that sounded like every other song. Daniel stewed about Archies doom comment. He wanted to save Jayla, Tommy, and even Meg. Who was going to save him from himself?

TWENTY-TWO

ARCHIE WOUND THEM AROUND many roads. He didn't know the numbered address by heart and even if he did, Meg doubted the GPS app would work in this area of Marion County. You wouldn't exactly call it the heartland. A lot of old tobacco farms with gray wood barns that kind of leaned just not as elegant as that tower in Italy.

After a biscuit and greasy hash browns, their passenger became a little more forthcoming. Mostly warnings about what Johnny Mudd would do to Daniel and Meg. Then his beating would come. His half-brother kept a backhoe behind his barn and legend has it a row of buried men in the soybean field. There was even a tiger in a cage on his property. He was a redneck James Bond villain.

Meg asked the right questions. Are there any alarms or traps on the drive up to the house? He thought there were some trail cameras set up. How many men were at the farm? He said anywhere from five to fifty depending on what was going on. Was there only one way in or out? He answered Johnny always had a back door anywhere he was. Was the law in his pocket? In all four pockets.

Archie pointed. "See that big rusty mailbox? That's it."

"Meg said, "There isn't any name on it."

"Johnny Mudd don't like to advertise. He's a snake. People only know they're near him when he rattles."

"For someone without a book in that big house of yours, you sure have a colorful way with words," said Daniel.

He crossed his arms. "I had a book."

"Bible doesn't count."

"Well, that's bullshit."

Meg pulled into the gravel driveway and parked once she was just off the road. A strip of yellow grass ran down the length of the drive they could see in the headlights. She twisted around to face the backseat.

"If he has cameras like this idiot says, we better gear up here." She opened the door and stepped out. She stepped back to Archie's door and opened it up. He leaned away from the brisk air.

"I got him." She took hold of his robe collar and drug him out of the Yukon. He stumbled then righted himself.

"These boots have a hole in them."

Daniel said, "You picked those boots."

"I was drunk and under duress. But no my right foot is soaked."

Daniel got out on his side and met them at the rear of the SUV. He raised the rear cargo door and got the floor panel hidden floor open. Meg's arsenal was packed in cut-out foam compartments. He heard Archie whistle.

"You brought the pepper. Maybe I was wrong about you two."

Meg said, "In that bag to your right are some zip ties. Had me one."

Daniel passed her a zip tie and Archie finally realized it was for him.

"Turn around and put your hands behind your back."

"Get the hell outta here with that. I'm drawing the goddamn line right now"

Meg just flicked the long plastic zip tie like she was swatting a fly on his crotch. She must have struck her target because he puckered his lips and bent over. She grabbed his left wrist and wrenched it behind his back. She threaded the zip cuff up his hand into place.

"Give me your other hand or I'm hitting your left ball this time."

He reluctantly stuck his left hand back. Meg roughly grabbed it and slid it into the cuff. She pulled both zips tight with relish then turned him around. She took him back to his rear seat and put him back in. Daniel selected the pistol he wanted and made sure it had ammo. He took a roll of silver duct tape and stuck it in his hoodie pocket. There was some kind of tactical vest in there too. He lifted a corner of it and it was too heavy for just cloth.

She said, "Hands off my bulletproof vest."

"Don't you think that's overkill?"

"Have you been listening to him tell stories about his brother the hillbilly Don Corleone? I should have brought a tank."

She took off her winter coat and slipped on the vest over her ribbed sweatshirt. A shotgun with a pistol grip and no shoulder stock was her next selection. She racked a shell then loaded five more shells with copper color pins into the underside. Five more shells in red plastic were in a side saddle holder on the side opposite the ejection port.

He looked at his plain black polymer pistol. "This all I get."

"You got that whole kung-fu Viking berserker thing," she said. "Shut the door and let's go get Jayla."

"I appreciate all the hardware but let's see what Johnny Mudd says first before you go all Annie Oakley." He closed the cargo door.

"I'll try not to blow his kneecap off while you are negotiating." She turned and rounded the rear of the SUV.

"Just don't blow my eardrum out," he said to the space Meg had occupied. He went to his rear right passenger side and got in. Archie squirmed into a semi-comfortable position sitting sideways.

"Assume he can see us approach so no need to come in spitting gravel."

She said, "Nice and slow it is."

She put it in drive and accelerated so fast she rocked Daniel and Archie back in their seat. As the car slowed, she laughed. "Hold on ladies."

He shook his head. He felt she was as nervous as him.

She flaunted her reckless nature to hide the fear but he sensed it leaking from her. If he learned anything in therapy, it was that what people say doesn't reflect their inner thoughts or emotions. You check their actions. This was where they revealed their true nature.

The luxury SUV drove like the uneven gravel ruts were soft shag carpeting. He was thinking he might have to upgrade his vehicle when he got home. If he got home. He hadn't planned too far ahead. Just been following any crumb his cousin left behind. Molly back at Huddle House kept drifting into his thoughts. Live in the moment. Let the past die. Don't worry about the future.

His future likely held violence. Would Molly want to be with him if she could see his true nature? He wasn't confident but the spark between them gave him hope that she already saw him. Truly saw him warts and all. Accepting what he had to offer and what he could never give. That's how he saw her. A person who was confident in her character not needing or heeding other outside influences. She just was.

He could make out a stone two-story farmhouse in the distance. A wooden plank fence ringed it. It wasn't far from a large garage whose interior was lit up revealing a Ford pickup truck, a late model Cadillac sedan, and a John Deere tractor. And there was still room in the garage for more vehicles. Behind the garage was a tall silo.

Further, back a pace from the silo he could make out a black barn. It didn't lean like the other barns he had seen throughout the county. It looked constructed better than the house. Barns had always been places of joy for him. This one gave him pause. Felt like it was watching their approach.

"Nice spread of land. What does he grow on it?"

Archie said, "Johnny? He doesn't grow anything on it. He leases the land off to a couple of farmers."

Daniel pushed him against the door. Every time he opened his mouth, he wanted to harm him. "What do they grow?"

Archie shrugged off the shove. "Tobacco, corn mostly. Some soybean. There is a little vegetable garden by the house that Johnny's gal plucks tomatoes from in the Summer."

Meg said, "No weed? I thought the KFM made their riches off pot."

"That's right but he ain't stupid enough to grow it on his property. Feds and task force been bird-dogging him for years. Hell, they might be out in the woods watching now."

"But not the local law right? The sheriff's folk work for him."

"Everyone likes money. Except the feds. Can't reason with those assholes."

"They ever arrested Johnny?"

"Not once. Out of fear or loyalty. His people don't talk. And nobody in this county witnesses anything."

Daniel hung a hand on the top of the front seat. "The King of Pot just sits on his throne unopposed. Does he have no enemies? No rivals?"

Archie shook his head. "He made his deal with the devils down South. I wouldn't call him and the Cartel friends but they have a bromance going on. Weirdest thing I ever saw. Spics in slick suits and Johnny in his denim coveralls watching cockfights together."

"How long has Johnny been in charge?"

"He started the whole business. There were always people running grass in Kentucky. But he started a group of mostly family members that steamrolled the competition. Get on board or get run over."

"Sounds very macho," Meg said from the front seat.

"People respect strength in this state."

Daniel dropped his hand from the seat. "Sounds like a bully."

He nodded. "Reckon he is. He's also generous to friends and family in need. Built the new high school gym when funding fell through."

They came to the fence surrounding the house and drove through an open gate. There were four vehicles parked diagonally in the grass off the drive near the main house. A telephone pole with long wires had an arm with a beaming lamp on it. Cast a sickly yellow glow down in the parking area. Meg swung out in the grass in a big circle facing the nose of the Yukon back out the way they came and parked.

"You two just going to go up and knock on the door of the most dangerous man in Kentucky in the middle of the night. That your plan?"

Daniel pulled the duct tape from his pocket and pulled a long strip off. "Pretty much except you're coming too. Once I tape your mouth shut."

"Johnny! Hey! Owww."

She reached over and grabbed a fistful of hair pulling him up straight. Daniel applied the tape strip to his mouth and smoothed it down sealing it off. He shook his head and tried to stretch his mouth to get the tape off. Daniel chuffed him under the chin and he banged his head into the hard window.

Daniel never felt like a bad man even when he lost control and hurt people. Now being bad was imperative. He accepted this role a little too readily. Some sessions with Dr. Rhiney exploring this new normal may be in order. Or a long walk with Molly might help too. These were options for later. Jayla and her son needed him at his worst.

She opened the door and got out with her shotgun. He got out and came around to her side of the SUV. She said, "Bust in the door. Shoot whoever gets in our way and get Jayla and Tommy."

"Or, we knock on the door and ask for Jayla."

She grimaced. "Even the dumbass thinks that's a shitty plan."

"It's unexpected."

She shook her head. "They'll think we're nuts."

"Exactly. Which puts them off balance. Gives us an edge."

"I'm not giving up my gun."

He noticed Meg trembling. "You keep your gun. We go in there guns a blazing we might hurt Jayla and Tommy. Let me talk first."

She opened the rear passenger door and Archie fell

on the cold grass. He had been pressed against the door trying to eavesdrop.

"Hear anything asshole."

When Daniel rolled him over his eyes were a little glassy and there was a knot on his forehead. There was a large stone on the ground where his head struck.

"Dammit. We need him in one piece."

She brushed Archie's hair back and inspected his lump. "He's fine. And quit yelling at me. You've been smacking him all night."

A deep voice spoke. "You all going to stand out here all-night grabbing ass or you going to come inside?"

Meg spun, racked her shotgun, and pointed it towards the voice. Daniel pulled his pistol and swung his aim in that direction too. A large shape was silhouetted by the porch light. The shapeshifted to one side and the light revealed a tall man with broad shoulders and a broader belly. He wore a white t-shirt under blue denim coveralls. A long mostly grey beard hung down to his potbelly.

"Come on in. Bring my piece of shit brother with you." With that utterance, he went around the rear corner of the farmhouse.

"It's a trap." They both said together. Still, he gathered Archie onto his wobbly legs and they followed after the legendary, Johnny Mudd. They entered a mudroom, not unlike his grandma's they had passed through earlier in the evening. Crossing this threshold felt more ominous than welcoming though.

The kitchen was expansive with a big wooden dining table with mismatched chairs. Some wooden back and a few from diners with cracked vinyl seats that had yellow foam peeking out. A light over the kitchen sink was the only illumination. Johnny Mudd stood in the doorway leading to the next room. He swung his big paw of a hand for them to follow him. There were no other people Daniel could see.

The next room was a living room of sorts. A worn leather wrap-around couch dominated the space. A cloth fabric La-Z-Boy recliner was the only other chair in the room. All the seating faced a ten-foot-wide flatscreen TV on the wall. On the screen was a boxing match featuring Ken Norton and Larry Holmes. Daniel knew that because the sports graphics text at the bottom of the screen was as big as his hand.

In the upper right corner of the screen was a picture-in-picture. This image wasn't of another TV show. Instead, he could see the Yukon they drove up to the house on it. Their giant host sat down in the recliner and pressed a button that made a whirring sound as it raised his feet. Daniel placed the still loopy Archie onto the couch next to him but chose to stand. Meg was at his left holding her shotgun in Johnny Mudd's direction.

"Sit. Take a load off." If he was nervous to have a gun pointed at him, Daniel couldn't tell.

"Where's Jayla?"

He smirked. "Down to business is it?"

"Is she here?"

He pulled out a large remote from the crease of the armchair. Pressed a couple of buttons and the small picture in the corner filled the whole screen. The hidden camera was a full-color monitor and captured the image in crystal clear resolution. A click and the screen jumped to a different view of the driveway. Another jump cut showed the rusty mailbox at the very front.

"I rarely get uninvited visitors. But you all are the second ones I've had recently." He had a green plastic cup filled with ice next to him and he took a drink from it.

"Where are Jayla and Tommy?"

"She tried to sneak in here and take that little fella. But as you can see it ain't easy to get the drop on me. Since I don't like to let my family stray too far, I couldn't let her have Tommy."

Meg kept checking the doors. Watching for any help that Johnny Mudd might have around. No one stirred.

Daniel said, "She didn't like that."

"Not one little bit. She started haggling for her kid."

"Haggling?"

"Negotiating really. First, offer she stuck a gun under my nose. I took that off the table pretty quick. My counter-proposal was that she works in my brothel and she could see the boy from time to time."

Daniel could feel his heat rising unbidden in his shoulders. "See his mom as a whore."

Johnny Mudd sucked his teeth. "Yeah, she wasn't keen on that option either. She said she could get me money if that's what I wanted. I laughed but she threw out a really high number off the bat for a poor piece of trash."

The heat in Daniel met the cold realization of his cousin's statement. "She was trying to play you."

He took another drink from his green plastic cup. He

rushed to speak before he finished swallowing. "That's what I thought too. But she kept insisting she could get it. Had made a big score."

Johnny Mudd leveled his granite glare at Meg then at him. No doubt he knew about their heist. She must have been too desperate for her son. He tamped down his fire. Daniel would need his cool to wriggle out of this mess.

"She's a strong woman. More grit in her than that sack of crap Archie. I asked where the money from the Bluegrass Sports Club was. Nothing for nothing she said. Give her Tommy and she'll give me her share."

He could sense Meg's finger getting tense on the trigger. He calmly placed a hand on the barrel and lowered it to the floor. Worse words were coming and they needed him alive to get Jayla.

"I wanted it all. But she won't spill any other details. Not even after some vigorous questioning. I did surmise an inside man was involved. Archie remembered her and Carl from the club being friendly. We brought him over. He gave up two other people but he didn't have any names. So how could I find them?"

Meg answered, "You waited for us to come to you."

He clucked and pointed his finger at her. "Bingo was her name-o."

"You want the money. We can give it to you."

"Of that, I have no doubt." He sucked on an ice cube from his drink.

Daniel shook his head. "Nothing for nothing."

Dropping the ice cube back in the glass, he said,

"You want Jayla and the kid for the cash. You got the money on you?"

"Be dumber than dog shit to ride up here with it wouldn't I?"

Johnny Mudd shrugged and made a face. "You ain't showed me your brains yet."

"True but tell me if I'm lying. I'll burn everything down until I get Jayla. Your money included."

The large man set the glass down and stroked his beard. "I expect you would try." He checked his Rolex watch and smiled. "Meet at the Bluegrass Club at 10 a.m. I'll have what you want and you better goddamn have what I want."

Meg said, "Let's do it now."

The smile vanished. "I said ten. Have to fetch her from the trailer. Clean her up. Girl's been earning back the money the way God intended women to. On her back."

Meg started across the room. Daniel grabbed her back. The big man in denim stood up to his full height from the chair. They were dismissed.

Daniel said, "Ten at the club. As good faith we'll leave Archie with you."

"Oh no. Take that dumbshit with you. One less thing I have to clean up."

"I thought you kept family close?"

"That apple couldn't have fallen farther from the family tree if he wanted. Take him and begone."

Daniel picked the concussed Archie up off the couch and took him through the doorway to the kitchen. He expected to be jumped by half the KFM when he stepped into the kitchen. No one waited. A clear exit path. Meg kept her shotgun steady on Johnny Mudd till they were at the back door. She walked quickly sideways to catch up.

She said, "You think he's just going to let us drive out of here."

"He's so confident we'll meet up that he probably filled our gas tank and inflated the tires." He got Archie into the back seat. He peeled the duct tape gag off and used his folding knife to cut the zip cuffs loose.

"Yeah, that asshole was unnerving. What do we do for…" She pulled her phone out and checked the time. "…six hours?"

"Head back to Grandma's for sleep I suppose."

He was about to close the door after he got Archie buckled in but he mumbled Jayla's name. He lifted the woozy man's chin. "What about her?"

Archie was crying. "He shouldn't have done that to my sweet Jayla."

Meg loaded the shotgun in the front seat. "You feel bad now? After all, you did to her."

"I didn't put her in no whorehouse."

"You let your brother have Tommy. You told Jayla who had her son. Sent her to death himself."

"But I didn't want her to get pimped out. That's…he talks about family. Family doesn't do that."

Daniel wanted to slap him so hard his muscles locked up. "It was okay if he killed her just not sex trafficking. That right?"

"You ain't seen this place. There are things worth than death."

Meg reached back in for her shotgun. "I'm tired of his mouth."

Daniel put a hand on her back to halt her action. "Archie, do you know where this place is?"

"The Happy Hollow Trailer Park? I know its whereabouts."

"Sit tight." He shut the door on him. And leaned close to Meg. "Why wait till ten when we can get Jayla right now?"

Meg nodded. "Snatch her away before the meet and split town. Hell, yeah."

"Jayla won't leave without Tommy."

"Shit. We'll still have to meet at the club. Mudd will be super pissed too."

"He doesn't seem like the guy to have his kingdom messed with. Got to be a way to use that against him." Maybe his time in Anger Management therapy could help suss out an opportunity to exploit.

"Climb in and figure it out on the way. We got our girl to go save."

He went around to his side and sat next to Archie. He would have to doctor up his cousin's ex-boyfriend who had finally become useful for once in his shallow existence. Meg steered the massive black SUV away from Johnny Mudd's farmhouse under the watchful eye of many hidden cameras.

TWENTY-THREE

THE HAPPY HOLLOW TRAILER PARK did not represent its name very well. Even in the dark, he could tell this wasn't a place to discover any mirth. Archie had filled in the back history on the fabulous place. It used, to be honest to god trailer park built in the late seventies. Nice new trailers with working folk and some families. The next residents were a little worse. That trajectory continued until the original owners got too old and too in debt to care about it anymore to pay taxes.

Johnny Mudd bought it cheap at a county auction. There was going to be a bidding war with some out-of-state real estate hawk's representative. It seems millionaires are heavy investors in trailer parks countrywide.

They jack up the rent because the poor people have nowhere else to go. One owner in Florida only rents to male sex offenders. This out-of-town shyster made a higher bid than Johnny Mudd so he sent a couple of country-strong rednecks to sit on each side of the man in a suit. Johnny's next bid was the last.

He flipped Happy Hollow into a crash pad for his sex trafficking. The sheriff's department was too busy driving new cars and boats to check out any complaints of prostitution or drug use. No one cared as long as it was out of sight. And the trailer park was back in undeveloped land that wasn't any good for farming. How the original owners got this scrubland into a usable living space was a marvel.

Daniel had taken in the nightmare landscape on the way up to the trailer park. The tree limbs grew at odd angles. Sweeping and reaching to the sides like they were at war with each other. The trailer park was in a valley bottom. Meg had turned off the headlights again and just used the running lights so they were coming cautiously downhill on Barn Road. He could make out about eighteen to twenty trailers in the dark. Some lot spaces were void of a trailer.

Some porch lights dotted the park but all the interior lights were out. They crossed an intersection with Silo Road. They kept straight on Barn Road and went through the center of the trailer park. Corrugated metal skirts on most of the old trailer. Some had crisscross wood lattice skirting. A lot of rusty exteriors. Half the trailers look abandoned. A very few others had vehicles parked in their driveways. Pickup trucks mostly.

Archie snored to his left. He said, "Do you remember which trailer Mudd's pimp is in, or do I need to wake up sleeping asshole?"

Meg peeked through her window then looked back across at the trailer on the other side of the road. "It's got a cardinal red door. And what did he say he drove?"

He said, "A big truck with a chrome stack exhaust."

Meg rolled her head one way then the other cracking her neck. "So, we look for a redneck ride and red door. I hate Kentucky."

"Don't kid yourself. Every state in the union has rednecks. New York City, California, and even your beloved Ohio." He looked down Barn Road for any chrome catching the runner lights from their car.

"We have the Northern Redneck. It's the Southern variety that you have to keep your eye on."

They came to a bent stop sign that had Silo Road on it. Only two choices were available to go right or left. Meg went right. There were no trailers to the left of them only a copse of mostly leafless trees. They edged up on another road to their right. Loft Lane. He motioned for her to keep driving on the road they were on. The Yukon rounded the corner and there sitting in a driveway was a big ass truck with chrome stacked exhaust. A late-model Toyota Camry parked behind it.

"I'm questioning the KFM's leadership." She put the SUV in reverse parking on the side of the grass and shut off the running lights.

"Wondering why their guard dog isn't parked at the entrance?"

She adjusted her toboggan. "Doesn't make any sense."

"When you're feared enough, I guess you can do whatever the hell you want."

"What's the play? Loud." She racked a shell in her shotgun. "Or sneaky."

"Stealth mode until we get ahold of him. Don't want him to shoot us or run. Either way, we don't find Jayla." He patted his pocket checking he still had his gun.

He got out and she followed him to the trailer. Would have been great if they could look in a window but the trailer sat too high off the ground to sneak a peek inside. No light was emitted from any of the uncovered windows though. Daniel took the top off a concrete birdbath in the side yard and hoisted the column onto his shoulder.

"What are you going to do with that? Bust down the door."

"I'm not a lock picker."

They crept up the three steps to a red door. He set down the heavy column and checked the doorknob gently. It was unlocked. She got low and pointed the shotgun at the door. He opened the door from the side and gave it a little push to swing inward. Meg signaled it was clear so he stepped through the doorway. Their eyes had adjusted to the night but the darkness in the trailer was another matter.

Light came in through the windows but not enough. Meg flicked a button and a beam came off the bottom of her shotgun barrel from an attached flashlight. A quick sweep of the interior living room and kitchen showed no one present. A couple of stacked Fat Tony's pizza boxes and empty beer bottles on the coffee table. A pretty nice leather couch and the obligatory widescreen TV. Messy but nice.

Daniel pointed to the rear of the trailer where the bedroom would be. She led the way since she had the light and the bigger gun. He held his pistol down by his leg. He didn't even remember when it came to be in his hand. The cold difference-maker in his palm. The heat was in his shoulders again but it wasn't going to explode this time till he needed it. He wouldn't let it.

She kept her light beam pointed on the floor. It was a short nap beige carpet they walked on. A couple of spots sunk under his footstep but no creaking as they approached a cracked open door at the end of the hallway. Someone snored in the bedroom. She pushed the door all the way open with her foot and stuck her head in quickly. Her head came back out and she had a quizzical expression. She took another peek then turned to him and smiled broadly.

"You got to see this." And she stepped inside the bedroom with her shotgun raised.

Daniel came into the room and backed her up by aiming in the same direction. Her beam of light revealed a slight man with ginger hair and a beard to match. Another man much heavier and hirsute snuggled up close to the redhead with his arm draped across his chest. Any exposed skin glistened in Meg's flashlight. There was a strong coconut scent in the air. She saw him sniffing.

"Coconut oil." She pointed at a bottle on the bedside table. "Smells like they emptied the bottle."

He screwed his face then made the Oh face connection. The little guy was the loud snorer. Daniel took the bigger man as the pimp slash guard of this prostitute park. Meg pulled out her cellphone. She said. "Let me take a couple of pics for blackmail purposes."

She took a few shots with the flash on and that didn't stir the men on the bed at all. She put the phone back in her back pocket and trained her shotgun on them again. "Okay wake up the lovebirds."

Daniel kicked the bed frame and the sleeping couple kind of jostled. He poked the bed and it gave like a bowl of firm Jello. A goddamn waterbed. He took out his folding knife and stabbed it into the rubber lining then dragged the serrated edge to widen the hole. He and Meg took a couple of steps back as the water gushed out. It had a chemically treated odor.

The two men started to sink into the bed. Finally, enough water pooled into the bed frame that they started to stir. The little guy who woke first realized he was sinking in water and started to thrash. This woke big hairy up and he rolled over trying to get out of bed. Meg racked her shotgun.

"Stay put lovebirds."

The shotgun's tactical flashlight revealed the wide eyes on both men. The redhead tried to hide under the soaking wet blanket. The big guy held both hands in front of him.

The little redhead said, "Who are you?"

Daniel responded, "You mean what do we want?"

A flit of anger across his eyes. "Okay. What do you want?"

Daniel looked at the big guy. "Right now, we want to speak with the man in charge of Happy Hollow's."

The redhead sucked on his teeth and said, "I'm the lucky one."

Meg said, "Johnny Mudd let a little queer in charge of his girls?"

The redhead said, "Do you let a fox watch your henhouse or a flaming rooster?"

"I hate that asshole Mudd but that's brilliant."

"You're going to love it when he catches you two." The little guy reached for the table drawer.

Daniel pointed his pistol at the redhead. "Don't."

"It's just my vape pen. That okay? I'm shaking like a leaf."

Daniel nodded for him to go ahead but the little guy didn't seem scared at all. He pulled out a vape pen like he said and took a little suck on it. A little vapor escaped from the corner of his mouth. Now the room smelled like mint and coconut oil. The mint vape pen reminded him of his cousin which brought him back to business.

"Which trailer is Jayla in?"

The redhead took another pull on his pen and let out a larger plume that obscured his face. This reminded Daniel of the hookah-smoking caterpillar in Alice in Wonderland. He said, "Jayla? Lots of girls here. You could have just paid instead of busting in here with guns. You and Butchalong Cassidy want a three-way?"

Meg said, "Quicker you tell us. Quicker you can refill your water bed and get back to screwing."

His bedmate said, "I know who you mean. Mousy blonde hair. Loads of attitude."

The redhead sighed. "I don't sleep with them for their brains."

The big guy made an 'oh shit' face. "Sorry, Reggie."

Reggie patted him on his thigh. A gentle gesture that torqued Daniel up. "What trailer is she in?"

"You two look tough but Johnny? He's so lethal when he breaths flies die. So, you gals go on and leave. Before you get hurt. Shoo." He puffed on his pen again.

Meg slipped her phone out of her back pocket and keyed the screen to life. "Funny you mention Johnny Mudd. We just left his place a little bit ago. He gave me his number too. I took a couple of shots of you two snuggling on my phone. How's about I sext him your pics?"

Reggie scoffed. "He knows who I am and what I do. Send away."

"I wasn't talking to you, Reginald. What do you say oh hairy one? Let Mudd know you like pitching for the other team?"

"She's in number eleven. With the purple trim."

Reggie put his face in his hand. "Scott. Goddammit. They were bluffing."

"I'm no fag but if Johnny saw me with you, I'm dirt."

"She's bluffing, moron. No way she has Johnny Mudd's number."

She winked at Scott. "Big ole bluff but thanks for the info."

Daniel said, "Now you are going to get up one at a time. And we're going to cuff and gag you. If you even look at me wrong, I'll take that pillow off the bed, hold it to your head and pull the trigger." He looked right at Reggie. "Am I bluffing?"

Reggie's mouth hung open. He shook his head.

"Good. Big guy first."

Scott slid out of bed naked as the proverbial jaybird. Meg made a face but had the zip cuffs ready. She threw a roll of duct tape on the bed's blanket and got to work cuffing the hairy naked man. She looked over her shoulder at Daniel. "We're getting too good at tying people up."

Daniel asked himself was he a bad man? A voice from deep down inside called out to him. Sometimes violence is the answer. This he could not deny.

They pulled the SUV up to trailer number eleven back on Barn Road. Since that guy Scott mention the purple trim, Daniel had noticed other bright garish colors on certain trailers. They must designate the ones the girls were in. Maybe purple meant blond and green meant brunette. Some perverse color-coding by that pimp Reggie.

They got out. She still had her shotgun but he kept his pistol in his pocket. Some of the other trailers had vehicles parked in their driveways. Overnight guests that paid for the full night experience he supposed. There wasn't any car in number eleven's driveway and for that he was thankful. He might murder a man he caught inside with his cousin unless Meg got to him first.

This door had a padlock attached to a latch on the door and door frame. Meg aimed at the lock with her shotgun. He halted her and gave the shush sign with his finger. He didn't want to rouse any customers. All these patriots in the country carried or had guns in their cars. He inspected the door hinges and surmised it opened inward. Be hard for someone to break the door open against the padlock and the door swinging in but to kick the door inwards should be easier. He took a step back and put a boot to the lower door hinge.

The door separated from the hinge a little. He repeated the action on the middle door hinge only he put more weight into it. Better result with more separation. Two more kicks and he butted the door with his shoulder and the door gave up. The carnage to the door took the edge off a little. He was nervous about seeing his cousin. Meg stepped in behind him and swung the flashlight on the tip of her shotgun around.

This place was dustier and messier than the redhead sentry's trailer. The couch in disrepair. La-Z-boy recliner leaning to the left. Even the TV was ten years old. Gigantic unlike the latest flat screens. It did have a DVD player. Porno DVDs were spread on the cheap laminate coffee table next to a full ashtray. He took a sniff of stale sweat, smoked cigs and dust. But no coconut oil thankfully.

Meg had started down the hallway without him. He called, "Wait."

She didn't slow down and was quickly out of sight. He heard a door open then pained exultation. He hot-stepped it down the hall to an empty doorway and Meg's shotgun on the ground. He pulled the gun from his pocket and pointed it towards the bedroom as he entered. Meg was on her knees at the bed holding Jayla's hand crying.

She said, "Look what they did to her."

He walked over and turned on the bedside lamp. The king-size bed took up three-fourths of the room. Jayla lay under the covers with her head exposed on a pillow. Their commotion and the light hadn't woken her. He slowly pulled the covers back, tracing down to her feet. She wore a pit-stained white cut-off tee shirt and panties. A chain was attached to a faux fur-lined cuff on her ankle. He swept the chain up into his hand searching for the anchor.

The chain was thick and long enough to have the roam of the bedroom. He found the anchor and it was solidly hooked into the floor. There wouldn't be any tools in the trailer to assist the prisoner to escape. He still didn't want to fire off the shotgun. The fewer half-naked men with guns the better.

"The Yukon have a pry bar?"

Preoccupied with trying to wake Jayla, Meg said, "What?"

"In the truck. Is there a pry bar or a crowbar?"

"There's a wheel wrench to jack it up."

He said, "That might work be right back."

"She's drugged up bad. Bring a bottle of water back."

He ran out of the trailer rushing to the rear of the SUV. He has to move some of her gear off the wheel well before lifting the floor panel. Next to the full-size spare tire was a jack and four-piece rod segments. Three connected to make one long bar then slid into a hole horizontally in the lug wrench to rotate the jack lifted the SUV. The lug wrench had a sharp tilted flat end that would work for him.

He took the lug wrench, stuck a bottle of water in his pocket, and left everything else open rushing to shut the rear door and get back to the bracket on the floor. As he turned to go, he glimpsed a blue cloth flapping in his peripheral vision. He fully turned his attention and saw Archie about ten feet away walking down Barn Road with his blue robe flapping open like a cape. Daniel gripped the lug wrench suppressing any thought of walking up and braining his cousin's ex with it.

"Where the hell do you think you're going?"

Archie just nonchalantly spun and cast up his right arm in salutation. "Just going for a drink. Woke up and no one was there. Not you who likes to hit me or the angry dyke. The JD bottle was empty too."

He tapped the lug wrench against his leg. "Want me to hit you again?"

"Hard pass." He lolled his head. "I'm not up for any more lumps."

"Then get your ass back in the car now." Daniel didn't wait for a response and headed back into the trailer.

Archie called from behind. "I'm thirsty."

He was at the broken trailer door but looked back at Archie pointed the lug wrench at him. "In the car now or under the car when we get done."

"Fine." Archie weaved in the direction of the Yukon.

In the bedroom, he tossed the water bottle on the bed next to Meg. Then he went right to the bracket anchoring the chain to the floor. Meg had Jayla sitting up on the edge of the bed. A sour smell came from her. He jammed the flat tip of the wrench between the bracket lip and the floor. Once wedged in he pushed with his arms. No wiggle. Whoever sunk the screws in had found a floor stud. He kicked the bent lug end of the wrench to wedge it in deeper. He climbed on the corner of the bed and jumped down with both boots onto the levered wrench. Kee-rack!

The bracket broke mostly loose. Another yank from him in the opposite direction and the chain was free from the floor. Meg tried to give his cousin a drink of water.

"Can she walk?"

"She hasn't said a word. Eyes barely open. What did they do to her?"

"We got to go. I'll carry her out. Grab the chain slack. We'll get to a hardware store and take it off her ankle later."

Meg just embraced her broken friend and lover. She kissed Jayla on her lips. This was when the fairy tale princess pricked by a poisonous thorn asleep for ages wakes from her stupor. This wasn't a Technicolor cartoon. Jayla slumped in Meg's arms.

He came over to the two women and unhooked them gingerly. He scooped up his cousin. He wasn't a large man and he was bushed but she felt lighter than an old aluminum lawn chair.

"Grab the chain. I don't want to trip."

Meg gathered up the loose chain and followed him out of the trailer. They reached the car and he put her on the rear passenger seat. Archie sat behind the driver's seat with a hangdog face. Daniel hitched his thumb at him. "Get out and sit in the front seat."

"This a trick? Trying to get me out of the car so you can run over me?"

He wished he had the lug wrench to strike him with. "Get out."

He did as commanded but not happily. Daniel said, "I'll drive. You take care of Jayla."

Meg's eyes were rimmed red from the salt of her tears. She handed him the Yukon key fob and she climbed in next to his ailing cousin. Archie still stood with his hands in his robe pocket outside the SUV. Daniel gave him a shove in the direction he wanted him to go. "Get your ass in the car."

Daniel got behind the wheel and pressed the button starting the powerful engine. His passenger slash hostage finally climbed up into the SUV cab and closed the door. He pulled at his robe. He reopened the door jerked his robe in then slammed it shut. Daniel was a hair away from murdering this man and he seemed oblivious to that fact.

He called over the front seat. "Hang on to her. I'm not that good a driver."

"Drive us straight out of Kentucky."

He accelerated out of the Happy Hollow Trailer Park up Barn Road. "We still have to meet Mudd in three hours. She wouldn't want to leave without her son."

"I know but I just want her away from all this. Take her home." She started to cry again.

"I'm taking us to the closest thing we have." He knew the way to their only sanctuary in Marion County. "We're going to Grandma's."

TWENTY-FOUR

SANCTUARY WAS GIVEN at the Durand family home. Grandma met them at the door and helped get her sickened granddaughter into the girl's bedroom. She raised twelve children in this old farmhouse. Seven women and five men. The second floor had two great rooms. All the girls slept on the north side and the boys on the south. Where the girls slept had two bunk beds, a queen-size bed, and one single.

Jayla rested in the queen-sized bed. Grandma sat in a rickety scarred high back wooden chair applying a cool rag to her forehead. A pitcher of water and glass on the nightstand. His cousin stirred a little at his grandma's nurturing. He felt better when her eyes finally creaked open and she asked for sweet tea instead of water. He went with Grandma to fetch some sweet tea and some biscuits from the kitchen downstairs. Meg took his grandmother's seat in the chair.

He came clean to his Grandma in the kitchen. It was only fair since their refuge with her might bring down the wrath of Johnny Mudd and the Kentucky Fried Mafia to her home. She listened to his whole tale without interjecting. Nothing was left out. He felt like this was his last confession and he must be absolved of all sins before he died. He choked up when he got to Jayla at the Happy Hollow Trailer Park.

She had put a tray of biscuits in the oven when they first came down. Tea was boiling in a pot on the stove. She said, "You always had each other's backs since you were little tykes skipping rocks and chasing chickens. Anyone mess with one of you they got the other cousin too. But Danny, this isn't little kid stuff."

"No ma'am it isn't. We'll leave as soon as we can. I don't want Johnny Mudd bothering you."

She tutted him. "He won't come here. I know his momma."

"I think a lot of men's mommas would disagree with you. There doesn't seem to be a boundary he won't cross."

"That is true. Still, I think you all are safe. Unless you go to that damn meeting." The tea had finished steeping and she filled her Tupperware jug with the hot liquid holding the tea bags back with her wooden spoon.

"Can't leave without Tommy. And we don't want that psycho nipping at our heels for the rest of our lives."

"You think he'll meet and trade fairly? Not a chance."

He gathered the hot biscuits from the oven. "No, he'll kill us, take the money and run Jayla to ground. Unless."

"Unless what?" She added her fourth cup of sugar to the tea and stirred,

His chin sunk to his chest. "I don't know. I've been winging it this whole time. He's smarter than me. Sure as hell has been doing dirty deeds longer than me. I've been trying to move fast and keep him off balance. Zig when I should zag."

She raised his chin. "Remember that mean ole rooster we had when you were a kid?"

"The one that used to attack you when you got eggs from the hen house. Yeah, he scared the crap out of me and Jayla."

"I sweet-talked him. Gave him extra feed. I warned him. I even had to shoo him away with a kick. None of that kept him from trying to spur me. You know how I finally got him to stop?"

He shook his head. And she said, "I cut the little bastard's head off."

She took her pitcher of tea up and walked to the staircase. Daniel got the biscuits and hurried to catch up to his Grandma and consigliere.

He was naked in a pit. There were mottled feathers on the ground as long as his forearm. The only source of light came from the opening above. He saw heads sticking over the edge to watch. Jayla, Meg, Dr. Rhiney, Grandma, and even Molly the waitress. He heard something scratch the dirt floor from the shadows. The shape concealed but then it moved forward into the light. It was a rooster the height of an ostrich.

Sharp yellow beak, impressive red wattle, and comb, long legs with a protruding spur. The rooster strutted towards him lowering its head and pumping its brown and amber wings. The flightless bird sprung high into the air rearing back to strike him with his long spurs. Daniel threw up his arms to catch the brunt of the kick and felt cold slashes deep into his muscles. The rooster bumped him to the ground with its broad chest.

His muses above cajoled him to fight back but his blood mixed the dry dirt into mud and he knew he was down for the count. The cock's black doll eyes measured the distance then a loud crow echoed as his throat feathers expanded out. The cock leaped high into the air once more. The last thing Daniel saw was the point of the spurs coming toward his eyes.

He woke up with his face scrunched in a pillow. He was on his stomach in one of the empty single beds next to his cousin. She was sitting up propped by pillows in her bed. Meg sat on her bed and Grandma in the bard back chair. Jayla gave him a weak smile.

She said, "Hello little snoozy."

He pulled himself upright and wiped the drool from the corner of his mouth. "How long was I out?"

"About an hour and a half. I conked out too. Your Grandma got me up when Jayla woke," said Meg.

He saw light out the window. "The meet. What time is it?"

She held up her hands. "Settle down. It's only eight forty-five. We got time."

He wiped the sleepers from his eyes with the palms of his hands then let out a big yawn. He fished his dark sunglasses from out of the covers and put them back on. Jayla patted the empty side of her bed. "Come here."

He sat down on her left side and she gave him a warm sideways hug. She still had a chemical odor to her but it was fainter than before. The weakness wasn't just in her smile. Her eyes didn't contain that glint he had always sought. This wasn't his same cousin. Maybe she never would be.

"Meg was just telling me your crazy plan to get Tommy." She stroked his bearded cheek.

"Plan? That's funny because I haven't even figured one out yet myself. I'm winging it just like you taught me." He put his hand over hers and felt how cold her fingers were.

"Thank you."

"You would've done it for me."

Her eyes welled up with tears. "I don't know if I could have."

He squeezed her hand. "You're so tough a snapping turtle wouldn't bite you."

She laughed through her tears. "That turtle had a hold of your shoe if I remember right."

"They were Chuck Taylors. You said just untie it and let it go."

"But you cried they were your favorites."

He nodded. "They were my only tennis shoes. I couldn't lose one to that turtle."

Meg said, "What did you do?"

"I kept tugging which was useless." He inclined his head towards his cousin. "She finessed the situation."

Meg scrunched up the skin between her eyebrows. "Finessed?"

He said, "She tickled the snapping turtle."

Jayla said, "Under its legs."

Grandma laughed. Meg shook her head. "You can tickle a turtle? You two should have had your own show on Animal Planet."

His cousin's face clouded up again. "Don't think tickling Johnny Mudd is going to get Tommy back."

He kissed her hand and rested it in her lap. "You'll be hugging Tommy before you know it. Trust me."

Her eyes fluttered and she began to fade into sleep. He got up and stretched his arms to the ceiling. The biggest yawn he had ever given stretched his jaw muscles to the limit. He first rolled his shoulders in the sockets a couple of times. Turned his head to the right to crack it and the left for a crack. Body unlocked, he looked at Meg.

"Let's go."

She gave Jayla a long kiss on the lips and met him at the bedroom doorway. Grandma sat guard by their broken sleeping warrior princess. "I can call your uncles if you need some help. Getting Tommy is all that matters. Selfish thinking it's your mess to clean up alone."

"My ego isn't in the way Grandma. If I thought Uncle

Earl and the others would help, I would take it. I think lean and mean is the way to go."

She leveled the Durand gaze at him. At both of them. "Can you do it?"

They both answered, "Yes."

She dismissed them with a choppy wave.

They floated through the house to the driveway and the Yukon Denali. Frost was on the windows. The sun hadn't broken through February's clouds yet. They got in the cab and she started the SUV bringing the defrost up to Sahara Desert heat. A mumbling came from the rear seat. Daniel checked and Archie was huddled on the seat with Meg's coat for a blanket.

He murmured, "I almost froze to death."

"Why didn't you come inside?"

"I don't like getting hit by wooden spoons."

"Not welcome huh? You could've run away."

"I'm miles from anywhere else. And didn't you say if I took off, the last thing I would see would be the underneath of this truck?"

Daniel scratched his beard. "I may have implied that."

He held his palms up and leaned up in Daniel's face. "So I waited here and froze. For you."

Daniel put his hand on his cold forehead and pushed him back into the seat. "You'll warm up you big baby."

The frost melted fast and they could see. Meg turned the SUV around and look the long gravel road away from Jayla, Grandma, and refuge. Time to see if they carried enough weight to pay the dues.

TWENTY-FIVE

DANIEL WALKED UP THE DIRT ROAD into the gravel parking lot carrying his big duffel bag by the shoulder strap. There were about five cars in the parking lot of the Bluegrass Sports Club. One was that familiar Dodge Charger with the QCKCAT vanity plate. That smiling prick Billy must be inside. Another Ford Expedition looked like an unmarked police vehicle. He could see the light bar behind the grill. The rest were pickup trucks of different models and years.

Outmanned and outgunned. He could hear Meg's voice inside his head as her fingers vibrated on the steering wheel. *This is your plan? Walk in and get killed.* She wanted to try and take Tommy by force. Maybe sneak in the back and surprise Johnny Mudd. They still had his cousin's key from their heist. He didn't want to risk little Tommy getting hurt if they had to shoot it out. She finally relented to his stupid scheme.

As he approached the club with the sun to his back, he saw movement at the door. A sentry had spotted him and came out to meet him aiming an AR-15 rifle at him. He halted and held his hands up as the broad-shouldered man with a brush cut talked into a handheld radio.

The sentry said, "Got one out here."

A squelch response asking who. The sentry responded, "Yeah, the ugly guy."

Another burst of squelch. The man with the rifle trained on him copied and put the radio in his pocket. Daniel saw two opportunities to take the rifle away while the man was talking on the radio. Decided to wait.

"Against the car. I need to search you for a weapon before we go inside."

Daniel went to the closest car and turned his back to the man. He slowly took the duffel bag off his shoulder with one hand and sat it on the ground next to him. The man came close and put his hands on him exploring any pocket for a gun or knife. Patted his belt line then ran both hands down his Carhartt work pants to his boots.

The guy stepped back. "Take off your hat."

Daniel complied and lifted his watch cap off revealing messy hair but nothing else. The man pointed his rifle at the duffel bag. "Open that up."

Daniel pulled his hat back onto his ears. "That's for Mudd's eyes only."

He pointed the barrel back at Daniel. "Unzip it fugly."

He picked up the duffel bag and hoisted it back on his shoulder. "Go ahead and shoot. Then have fun with the boss after he finds out you looked at his private stuff."

He plucked his radio back out and keyed it. "He's clean but he has a big duffel bag. Doesn't want me to look inside."

A loud squelch response. The guy tilted his head away from the sonic blast. "Copy that. We're coming in."

He swept the rifle for Daniel to move inside. He opened the door and went inside. The club's entryway was dark. He could see light leaking from the doors leading to the cockfighting arena. The man nudged him with his rifle barrel to keep stepping.

"Pick it up. He's waiting by the pit."

Daniel pushed open the double doors and walked through into the arena proper. The place wasn't completely lit up. Only the elevated cockfighting pit had full illumination. Why they called it a pit when it was above ground, he didn't know. One thing was sure, you couldn't scrub out the poultry smell completely. Or the stain of chicken shit and blood on the dirt floor. Scoop up the filth. Spread out fresh dirt.

There were twenty men in the arena. A few sat in the stadium seats surrounding the chicken wire caged pit. Johnny Mudd stood in the center of the pit in all his denim glory. He had a red bandana tied around his head. Going for that buccaneer farmer look. Six stout fellows formed a semi-circle behind him. Jeans, sweatshirts, and hoodies mostly. One guy he assumed was a deputy had on a tan tactical vest and some small automatic rifle secured to his rig. Like something out of a video game, Daniel had played.

All the other men had tricked out AR-15 rifles. The obligatory mascot of the Kentucky redneck shitkicker. The leader of the KFM had his long arm around the shoulders of a man Daniel couldn't fully see. He didn't see Jayla's kid Tommy anywhere. As he got closer, he saw the man next to Johnny Mudd was Reggie from the Happy Hollow Trailer park. The red-headed pimp's right eye was swollen shut. Bruised pinch marks on his lips and nostrils from pliers most likely.

He hadn't any fondness for the man who guarded his cousin but that abuse from a bully triggered Daniel. He felt the flush of heat rising. His ears roasted hot. If he didn't hurry up and make his deal, he might throttle past the point of no return. Tamping back the rage but keeping it close to the surface, he said, "Where's Tommy?"

He let go of the little redheaded pimp. "I was just talking to Reggie about you. Was explaining why Jayla wasn't there when I came to pick her up for our exchange. Said you had some nice moves."

"I got moves, Danny boy." He snapped his fingers and the off-duty deputy handed him a manilla file folder. Johnny opened it, licked his fingers, and pulled apart some pages. "Daniel J. Brown. Date of Birth 2/20/1987, height 5'11", weight 170lbs. Father unknown. That's a shame. Boy needs a male role model. Mother's name is Carla Durand. She was a sweet piece of meat back in the day. Says your eyes are blue but you always have those big black shades on. Come on let me see your baby blues, Danny boy?"

He adjusted the duffel bag on his shoulder. "You want your money? Let me see Tommy."

Johnny Mudd held up his big bear paw. "Lots of juvenile shenanigans. Says you have some diagnosed intermittent explosive disorder along with minor assaults. This last altercation was a doozy though. Still on probation for it." He shut the file folder and handed it back to the deputy who stepped back into formation.

He squinted at Daniel. "Even I saw that on the news when it happened. You turned into the goddamn wolfman on those guys. Savage. I was impressed."

Daniel waited him out.

"Since you and your partner decided to renegotiate, I thought it would fine for me to propose a counteroffer of my own."

His fingers were tapping at the shoulder strap. "You keep Tommy. I give you the money. And I go to jail since you own the law in Marion County."

The big man smiled through his yellowing beard and mustache. "Something like that. Is that my money in the bag?"

He took it off his shoulder and held it out. "Something like that."

Johnny shoved the beaten redhead forward. "Fetch."

Reggie limped over and took the duffel bag from his hand. A look mixed with hate but also pleading for help came from his one open eye. So weak he could barely hold the bag that he had to drag the money back to his master. Johnny Mudd patted his cur on his head and bent down to unzip the bag. He peered inside and looked up to Daniel with murderous intent.

"Smelly clothes and a tire jack. Not a smart play, Danny boy."

He pointed back to the bag. "You forgot about the phone. Swipe it awake."

Johnny Mudd reached in and took out a smartphone. He glanced at Daniel then swiped his thick finger across the glass face. His beard lit up from the glow. Mudd's brow furrowed and his eyes narrowed.

"This some kind of joke. I will bury you under the county jail if I don't get my money! Then I'll round up your trashy cousin and her pet dyke. Stick them back in Happy Hollow and send forty truckers to visit." He threw the phone into Daniel's chest and it ricocheted to the floor cracking the screen.

Daniel picked it up and tenderly swiped the cracked screen alive. He held up the live video feed so Johnny Mudd could see it. Meg had a cigar torch lighter on full blast next to a stack of money. "Bring Tommy out now."

Johnny Mudd's lips were so tight they looked like a razor slice. "You think this is only about the money?"

"It can't be solely about the money since I'm only giving you half the take. The rest is your and KFM's rep."

Mudd put his fingers to his temple. "You're dancing with the devil son. The song's almost over."

"You plan to kill us and take the money. You get the money and send a message to other thieves."

"It's a solid plan. Still don't see a need to change it. You're just dragging out the inevitable."

He held a finger up. "I think that too. You have a long reach and there isn't a line you won't cross. Can't fend you off forever."

"And still you think you're in a position to negotiate. Burn my money. I'll make it up by the end of the month. You'll still be dead. Your cousin Jayla? Dead. Anyone that helped you? Dead."

The men behind Johnny Mudd looked bored. One looked at his feet and another soldier in the KFM yawned. None seemed on edge or worried about Daniel. They were just waiting for the order to take him. Time to pitch his offer before Johnny Mudd snapped his fingers again.

"I noticed you liked my file."

"I appreciated your capacity for mayhem."

"Just between us. Have I been tough to deal with?"

"Been a pain in my ass. You don't act accordingly."

"But I impressed you didn't I? Just a little." Daniel held a little space open between his thumb and index finger.

The big man laughed. "Yeah. You're like those guerilla insurgents I watched on the Military Channel. Fast, mobile, unpredictable. Able to cause chaos and disorder to a bigger military force."

"I could be your One Man Guerilla Army."

He screwed up his face. "I'm listening."

"In return for Tommy and leaving everyone else alone, you get all the money we have left and me."

"You?"

"Not forever but I work off the money we owe you."

"This whole thing has been a job interview? Unbelievable. You want to work in the Happy Hollow trailer park?" He bellowed with laughter. He turned expecting his men to be laughing with him but they caught on late and their jeers and guffaws rang false. "Shut the fuck up."

"I'll do the nasty, ugly jobs where you need to send a message. No innocents. That's my line."

He stabbed a thick finger in Daniel's direction. "Fuck your line."

Daniel had struck a big throbbing nerve. The leader of the KFM stroked his beard for a moment then tilted his gaze towards Daniel. "I need to check your qualifications."

"How do we do that?"

"I'm going to step out of the cage. Then if you can take out everyone else inside, I'll consider not killing you and your friends." He made for the door out of the caged pit. The beaten Reggie limped after him until Johnny Mudd registered him. He shoved the pimp back until he fell in the dirt. "Collect all the guns then you can come out."

The other six men woke up and started to fidget with their rifles. Johnny Mudd snapped thunder from his fingers and each man handed what had to be a prized possession over to Reggie. He hooked a couple of the rifles on his shoulder then gathered the rest in his arms and stumbled out of the cage as fast as he could manage. The men started to spread out around Daniel.

"This is pretty lame."

"You said you were fast on your feet. A real outside-the-box thinker. Let's put that to the test."

Daniel didn't feel the fire rising. Summoning his rage on command was something he had been working on while he helped Jayla the first time in Marion County. In the last five months, he had kept himself under control. He didn't feel like losing control in this cage for Mudd's interview. He had gotten this far by not doing what was expected of him. At that moment he decided not to give the crime boss what he wanted.

That's when the deputy drove a heavy fist into his right ear. Daniel rolled with the punch and spun into a defensive posture. Blood rushed back into his flattened ear and the nerves sang out in pain. The deputy jabbed twice and threw a haymaker with his left. Daniel slipped it and pushed his opponent down into the chicken wire fence. It was made to contain small angry roosters, not a two-hundred-pound man and the deputy got folded up in the wire. Daniel had a smidge of hope that evaporated when another redneck tackled him down to the dirt floor.

The guy piled on top and rained blows down on Daniel's arms trying to split the seam and break his jaw. Daniel rolled and tried to buck the man off with his hips. Nothing doing. He reached up with both hands hooking them behind his assailants' neck and pulled himself up close taking the punch range away. Daniel then lurched backward and simultaneously popped his hips rolling the man over Daniel's head and onto his back. He rode Johnny Mudd's lackey around then jumped up and away once the roll was finished.

"I didn't say fight him one on one idiots. Drop his ass!" Johnny Mudd called from the VIP seats near the pit. He had his legs crossed and his arms across the seats. All he needed was some popcorn and a cold beer.

The other four goons mobbed him while the fellow on the ground snared his legs. They drove Daniel off his feet and dog-piled on top. Ten fists of fury couldn't be stopped or slipped. He ate a bunch of punches. The dam holding back his rage began to crack. His shirt tore in the melee. If he could just catch his breath to think. His glasses flew off in another wild swipe. And the dam broke.

He sunk his teeth into the first piece of exposed flesh he saw. He clamped down on the redneck's meat between the neck and the shoulder. He tried to make his incisors connect through the tough skin and sinew. The guy howled and jerked like a fish on a hook. Daniel let go and pushed with both his feet to dive out through the slim opening. No longer under the four men, he rose to his feet.

Usually, he was on autopilot and barely remembered this fugue battle state until he saw the aftermath. This time his instincts were still in control but he was fully aware. He licked at the blood on his lips. The four men looked wide-eyed as he breathed in deeply lifting his chin as he did so. The tang of fear was in their body odor. His hyper senses picking up all non-verbal messages now.

He heard a boot slide on dirt before he saw the man move. Daniel's kick caught the man's knee right when he planted his foot on the ground. The bent inwards accompanied by a sickening pop. That man wasn't on the ground before he swung a long arcing palm slap into the next goon's ear hole. Daniel scraped his nails across his cheeks for good measure. He let his momentum carry him into a roll then whipped his shin into the next closest man's ankles sweeping him off his feet. The guy sat straight up and Daniel pulled an uppercut into his chin so hard the guy's teeth clapped together. A broken castanet.

The leader of the Kentucky Fried Mafia clapped from his VIP booth. This was what Johnny Mudd wanted. The savage unleashed. He hadn't wanted to give Mudd what he craved. That's the intersection where you lose to this man. You can never let him have total control. His puppet strings are in your back. Daniel flowed with his violent current now. He would worry about unbalancing the evil son of a bitch after he laid these men down.

Two down, one ready to topple which left three more. The deputy had untangled the chicken wire and looked like he was reaching behind his back for something. Fear brings survival instincts. Johnny Mudd said no guns but when the deputy brought out a fixed blade knife, Daniel wasn't surprised. His savage nature detected the deputy as the highest threat and already had him in motion before he had pulled free his blade.

Daniel jammed his right forearm into the deputy's bicep simultaneously slapping his left forearm down on his wrist. He latched on the arm where his hands fell and twisted as hard as he could trying to separate the arm from the shoulder joint. The deputy used his free hand to try and push Daniel's body off of him. Another thug took this opportunity to slip an arm under his neck to choke him. He sunk on his knees a little and pulled the deputy's outstretched knife into the strangler's thigh. A large slash cut through the blue jeans and meat of his leg.

The strangler let go of his chokehold and held onto his gaping wound. One more out of the fight. The deputy wrenched his knife had free and, in the process, sliced the inside of Daniel's forearm. His hoodie sleeve took much of the cut but he could feel the cold burn in a length up to the elbow. The deputy flipped the blade into an ice pick grip. Daniel was tackled in the side by the sixth man who attempted to pull him to the dirt floor. Daniel sprawled his legs wide to keep from being taken down.

The deputy slipped to his other side keeping his knife hand up. The blade edge facing Daniel. He slipped a guillotine choke on the assailant trying to wrestle him to the ground but kept his eyes on the deputy's hips. A man can feint with his eyes but the hips always gave away the real plan. His hips pushed forward and Daniel levered the man in his chokehold off his feet. He swung him in the path of the deputy's charge.

The deputy halted his stabbing arc to miss his fellow KFM member. Daniel released his choke and grabbed the knife hand pushing the blade down into the other man's back. He let go and the deputy immediately pulled it back out. Daniel grabbed the hand again sinking it into the man's back. He danced back and pulled the deputy's arm toppling the two men down. Daniel stepped forward and kicked the prone deputy's jaw sideways. And the deputy went lights out.

Daniel stood with his hands hanging down at his side. Sweat soaked his hoodie making it heavy. He felt warmth in his right forearm from the slash he took. Blood trickled down his arm dripping off his fingers. He inspected the wound and found though it bled a lot it was superficial. The lights seemed to dim and the sounds muffled. His senses reverting to their normal states. God help him, Daniel was starving.

"Four minutes and thirty-six seconds. You did not disappoint Danny boy." Johnny Mudd climbed the steps into the cage. "Brutal, brutal, brutal."

"I'm not much with a gun." Daniel slung some blood from his arm then wrapped the cut sleeve into a bandage around the wound.

Johnny Mudd had picked up his sunglasses. "I got plenty of fools that can shoot. Now I got my own Tasmanian Devil."

"We got a deal?"

"Welcome aboard." Johnny Mudd handed Daniel his dark glasses back.

He slid the frames back on and pulled up his hood. "Can we get the rest of the deal over?"

Johnny Mudd detached the two-way radio from a pocket on his denim overalls. He spoke into the mic. "Bring out the boy."

A squelch response of assent. Johnny Mudd held his arm out to shepherd Daniel out of the caged pit. The adrenaline dump made him very tired all of a sudden. Crashing his nervous system except for his sliced arm. That burned like a son of bitch.

"Reggie, get some of the other boys to help you clean up this mess." Johnny hitched his thumb over his shoulder.

The beat-up redhead yelled at some of the guys sitting in the stands to give him a hand. Johnny Mudd walked by Daniel's side now once they were out of the ring. Two men escorted Jayla's little boy Tommy out from a door towards the betting booth in the arena. He walked between the goons holding both of their hands. They didn't rush the tyke. Tommy had a big grin on his face then waved at his evil Uncle Johnny.

Tommy stretched his arms out and his uncle picked him up. "Hey, kiddo. This is your Mom's cousin so that makes him your second uncle or is that second cousin. Shit. Say howdy-do, Tommy."

The little one held up his hand. "Hi."

Daniel mirrored his wave. "Hello."

"How do you want to do this?" asked Johnny Mudd.

Tommy hi-fived Daniel's hand. "I'll call Meg. You, I, and Tommy go out front and wait. Alone."

"Sounds simple."

Daniel walked through the double doors out of the arena holding one side open so, Johnny Mudd carrying the little boy could make it safely. The walk down the hallway to the exit was filled with Mudd's baby talk with Tommy. That was disconcerting. A sociopath cooing to a wide-eyed sinless toddler. What has his world become where the mundane and the obscene regularly intersect? He wished he could talk it out with Molly the oracle from Huddle House. Her vision might soothe him.

They exited the building alone. He got out the cracked cellphone and rang for Meg. One ring and she answered. "It worked. Park where we planned."

He ended the call. Johnny Mudd smiled at little Tommy but spoke to Daniel. "You think you're ready to work for me?"

"I'll do what I said."

"Even breaking the most unholy of holy commandments?"

Daniel stared hard at Johnny Mudd. "I'm not going to heaven anyway."

"Kid, Hell ain't so bad. Can learn a lot of new tricks down here."

"A man never stops evolving."

"Till he dies. And he starts dying once he leaves the warmth of his momma's womb. Then it's all scrapping and surviving till the end comes. We take from others so that we can live." He booped the toddler's nose. "Even little Tommy is a taker. How is that evil?"

"I'm cold," said Tommy.

Daniel forgot it was winter. He had forgotten all the seasons. His season was to get Jayla and Tommy free. He took off his Carhart jacket and wrapped it around the little tyke. Johnny Mudd helped him fit it around. He had another wide smile for Daniel when they were done swaddling the boy.

"What?"

"He just took your coat and proved my point. Tommy's defenseless. No fangs or ragged claws to fight or hunt with. But he's cute and pulls at your parental instincts. We cloth and feed him. We watch out for him. Call it God, evolution, whatever grand designer that gives us tools to use. Your tool is that berserker inside."

Daniel patted the jacket on Tommy and stepped away. "You think that's what got me this far? That rage and violence? Then I got something to teach you as well."

Headlights shone from the direction of the entry road into the parking lot. The Yukon Denali wove into the parking lot like a sleek killer whale. Meg parked in the back of the lot near the exit as they discussed. He said, "I'll walk Tommy to the SUV. Archie will walk the money over to you. You check it out. Give me the thumbs up and I'll give Tommy to Meg and come back."

"You going to skedaddle once you get over there?"

"I gave you my word. Besides if I tried that you would have that toothpick chewing idiot Billy gun me down from his hiding spot in the woods." He pointed to the Dodge Charger.

Johnny Mudd grinned. "Billy's a good soldier but that stupid fucking license plate will be his downfall."

He held his arms out for Jayla's son. Johnny handed him over. "I'll keep my word. Until I don't have anything else to lose."

Johnny Mudd gave him a short salute. He rubbed his hands together, pulled out a small cigar from his breast pocket, and lit it. The sweet burning of tobacco carried across the parking lot as Daniel carried the little boy. Tommy tucked his head down on his shoulder. His little foot digging into his injured forearm. Daniel was too concerned about shielding the kid from Billy's crosshairs to care about the pain.

He reached the SUV without a bullet in his back. A sigh escaped with the breath he had been holding the whole way across the parking lot. Meg rolled down her window. Archie climbed out of the car from the rear seat with the duffel bag full of cash. He came over and rubbed his son's head. The little fellow said, "Hi Daddy."

Archie ever the emotional one teared up. "Hey, buddy. You okay? Having fun with Uncle Johnny?"

"I hungry."

He wiped his eyes. "You are? Well, this nice lady is going to take you to McDonald's. You like Mickey D's right?"

The little boy's eyes lit up. "Mickey D."

She waved at him. "Hey, Tommy. I'm Meg. Want to come with me for some pancakes?"

"Pamcakes!" He kicked in Daniel's arms.

"Come on in and we'll go." She held her arms out for him.

Daniel handed Tommy feet first through the window. The kid slid in like one of the Duke boys of Hazzard County. He slapped Archie on the back. "Take that bag over to your brother."

"Can't I say bye to my son?"

Daniel turned his head scanning the woods. He scanned to Johnny Mudd and the small puffs of cigar floating over his head. He said, "Make it quick or your pal Billy will put a bullet in you."

Archie looked skittish. "Billy's here?"

"In the tree line somewhere. Go on and say bye."

Emotional with a helping of self-preservation kept the goodbye to his son short. Archie marched across the lot wearing his iridescent blue robe in untied sloppy boots.

Better than walking barefoot in winter on sharp gravel. The walk seemed so slow. Daniel thought about his dream. Of all the women looking down at him in the pit.

Jayla, Dr. Rhiney, Meg, Grandma, and Molly from the diner. He dreamt of a woman he had barely met but had seen him like no other. All those women had comforted him, given aid, given counsel, given themselves to him in friendship. His Mom wasn't watching with them. She wasn't in his dream at all. All those wonderful women on his side and all he thought about was how his Mom wasn't there.

Archie reached his destination. He dropped the bag at his large brother's feet. Johnny Mudd looked down then at his half-brother a second before slapping him hard in the face. The slap rocked Archie on his heels but he bent down and unzipped the bag spreading it open. Johnny Mudd looked down nodded his head at the money inside. He stared across the lot at Daniel a little too long.

He moved his cigar to the corner of his mouth and smiled. A big thumbs up came from the bearded country crime lord. Daniel let out his breath and waved back. Meg said, "Coolio. Get in and we'll split to Grandma's."

Daniel turned around and put two palms on the window sill. "I'm staying."

"What the hell? We got Tommy. Let's go."

He rubbed his nose. "I made another deal. One that will keep everyone safe."

"What did you do Daniel?" She grabbed his left hand that he left on the window.

"He's not going to kill me. I'm going to work for him. Just till I pay off what we took."

She scoffed. "He's like one of those school loans with twenty percent interest. You'll never pay him off."

He said, "You got to leave me here. And don't bring Jayla back looking for me. This is what I want."

Meg got weepy. "I can't stop her."

"You can now. After that shit with Happy Hollow. You and Tommy can help her heal. But you have to go back to Canada. Leave and never come back."

"How will we get in touch?"

He handed her the cracked phone. "We don't."

She kissed his cheek.

He patted the car door and said, "Take care of them, Meg. That's what will keep me going."

He turned and began walking back to the club before she could say anything else. He heard the gravel roll beneath the Denali's heavy tires. He didn't look back. He kept striding towards his new life. Life without rules and laws and love. He wondered how Molly would look at him when she saw him around town. All he had left were choices of violence. He belonged with Johnny Mudd and KFM now. He was alone.

ACKNOWLEDGMENTS

THIS NOVEL WAS INSPIRED by two branches of the same tree. This quote is from a Boris Karloff character in a 1935 film called The Raven. This killer was driven to a life of violence by his unseemly appearance. "Ever since I was born, everybody looks at me and says, 'You're ugly.' Makes me feel mean." I twisted that together with the French term Jolie Laide which translates to "pretty-ugly" or "good-looking ugly". A belief that even someone with a distinctive unattractive appearance by society's norms can still be beautiful. Can still find peace.

Firstly, I would like to thank Ron Earl Phillips and the Shotgun Honey family for allowing me to publish one of my mad dreams.

Thanks to my beloved Cord. Always an oasis in these troubling times. Outstanding people each and every one. This group literally saves my sanity daily. I wouldn't have the amount of success in my writing career without my Cord family.

The NBSCers James DF Hannah, Curtis Ippolito, and Holly West. It's going to happen.

Other writers who get special thanks are Scott Von Doviak, Meagan Lucas, C.W. Blackwell, Bobby "Top Bunk" Mathews, Mary Thorson, Ilyn Welch, Zakariah Johnson, Duane Swierczynski, S.A. Cosby, Paul J. Garth, Morgan Sullivan, Amina Akhtar, the original beta reader and Abysmal Brute Bill Wertenberger, the RHP team. And to all the other unnamed writers who give me support and community. The kindness of writers is always humbling.

To my brothers Gary and Chris. Sorry for being a smart-ass your whole life.

To my nieces and nephews Simon, Olivia, Avery, Nora, and Liam for allowing me to be the Funcle.

To all of my parent's enormous families the Smiths and the Filiatreaus. Growing up with all of them left a generous mark on my soul.

To my friends: my other brother Sean Rhiney, Tom Hubbs, Rocko Jerome, Mike Sadolsky, Dan Malmon(honorary Cord member), Matt Mitchell, Lori Driskell- forever friend and worthy first reader. You make me laugh. You make me question myself. I'm a better person for your continued support and friendship.

To Kentucky especially the counties of Nelson and Washington. The farm in Bardstown and the town of

Springfield were the playgrounds of my youth. Every memory hand written on my DNA.

ROB D. SMITH is a common man attempting to write uncommon fiction in Louisville, KY. His work has appeared in Apex Magazine, Shotgun Honey, The Arcanist, Pyre Magazine, Bristol Noir, Thriller Magazine, Thicker Than Blood, Tough, Vautrin, and several other crime, horror, and speculative anthologies and online magazines. He also edits at Rock and a Hard Place Press. Find more about him at https://robdsmith.carrd.co/

ABOUT
SHOTGUN HONEY BOOKS

THANK YOU FOR READING *Good-Looking Ugly* by Rob D. Smith.

Shotgun Honey began as a crime genre flash fiction webzine in 2011 created as a venue for new and established writers to experiment in the confines of a mere 700 words. More than a decade later, Shotgun Honey still challenges writers with that storytelling task, but also provides opportunities to expand beyond through our book imprint and has since published anthologies, collections, novellas and novels by new and emerging authors.

We hope you have enjoyed this book. That you will share your experience, review and rate this title positively on your favorite book review sites and with your social media family and friends.

Visit ShotgunHoneyBooks.com

SHOTGUN HONEY
FICTION WITH A KICK